THE PEARL
and
BURNING BRIGHT

'John Steinbeck, that tremendous genius.'—H. G. WELLS.

'He possesses subtlety, insight, and, above all, that simplicity of spirit which is the most distinguished feature of a true poet.'—RICHARD CHURCH in *John o'London's Weekly*.

'His just understanding of character, the candour and forcefulness of his dialogue and his mastery of climaxes are all his own and inevitable.'—*Times Lit. Sup*.

THE PEARL
and
BURNING BRIGHT

JOHN STEINBECK

UNABRIDGED

PAN BOOKS LTD : LONDON

By arrangement with
WILLIAM HEINEMANN LTD
LONDON

'The Pearl' first published 1948, 'Burning Bright' 1951,
by Wm. Heinemann Ltd.
This volume published 1954 by Pan Books Ltd.,
33 Tothill Street, London, S.W.1.

330 01308 4

2nd Printing 1955
New Edition (re-set) 1959
4th Printing 1963
5th Printing 1964
6th Printing 1965
7th Printing 1965
8th Printing 1966
9th Printing 1968

PRINTED AND BOUND IN ENGLAND BY
HAZELL WATSON AND VINEY LTD
AYLESBURY, BUCKS

THE PEARL

'Written with a tense and beautiful simplicity in which every word tells.'—*Birmingham Post*.

'This little masterpiece must stand out as a great achievement in simplification and sincerity.'—*News Review*.

'IN the town they tell the story of the great pearl—how it was found and how it was lost again. They tell of Kino, the fisherman, and of his wife, Juana, and of the baby, Coyotito. And because the story has been told so often, it has taken root in every man's mind. And, as with all retold tales that are in people's hearts, there are only good and bad things and black and white things and good and evil things and no in-between anywhere.

"If this story is a parable, perhaps everyone takes his own meaning from it and reads his own life into it. In any case, they say in the town that . . .'

I

KINO awakened in the near dark. The stars still shone and the day had drawn only a pale wash of light in the lower sky to the east. The roosters had been crowing for some time, and the early pigs were already beginning their ceaseless turning of twigs and bits of wood to see whether anything to eat had been overlooked. Outside the brush house in the tuna clump, a covey of little birds chittered and flurried with their wings.

Kino's eyes opened, and he looked first at the lightening square which was the door and then he looked at the hanging box where Coyotito slept. And last he turned his head to Juana, his wife, who lay beside him on the mat, her blue head-shawl over her nose and over her breasts and around the small of her back. Juana's eyes were open too. Kino could never remember seeing them closed when he awakened. Her dark eyes made little reflected stars. She was looking at him as she was always looking at him when he awakened.

Kino heard the little splash of morning waves on the beach. It was very good—Kino closed his eyes again to listen to his music. Perhaps he alone did this and perhaps all of his people did it. His people had once been great makers of songs, so that everything they saw or thought or did or heard became a song. That was very long ago. The songs remained; Kino knew them, but no new songs were added. That does not mean that there were no personal songs. In Kino's head there was a song now, clear and soft, and if he had been able to speak of it, he would have called it the Song of the Family.

His blanket was over his nose to protect him from the dank air. His eyes flicked to a rustle beside him. It was Juana arising, almost soundlessly. On her hard bare feet she went to the hanging box where Coyotito slept, and she leaned over and said a little reassuring word. Coyotito looked up for a moment and closed his eyes and slept again.

Juana went to the fire pit and uncovered a coal and fanned it alive while she broke little pieces of brush over it.

Now Kino got up and wrapped his blanket about his head and nose and shoulders. He slipped his feet into his sandals and went outside to watch the dawn.

Outside the door he squatted down and gathered the blanket ends about his knees. He saw the specks of Gulf clouds flame high in the air. And a goat came near and sniffed at him and stared with its cold yellow eyes. Behind him Juana's fire leaped into flame and threw spears of light through the chinks of the brush-house wall and threw a wavering square of light out the door. A late moth blustered in to find the fire. The Song of the Family came now from behind Kino. And the rhythm of the family song was the grinding-stone where Juana worked the corn for the morning cakes.

The dawn came quickly now, a wash, a glow, a lightness, and then an explosion of fire as the sun arose out of the Gulf. Kino looked down to cover his eyes from the glare. He could hear the pat of the corn-cakes in the house and the rich smell of them on the cooking-plate. The ants were busy on the ground, big black ones with shiny bodies, and little dusty quick ants. Kino watched with the detachment of God while a dusty ant frantically tried to escape the sand trap an ant lion had dug for him. A thin, timid dog came close and, at a soft word from Kino, curled up, arranged its tail neatly over its feet, and laid its chin delicately on the pile. It was a black dog with yellow-gold spots where its eyebrows should have been. It was a morning like other mornings and yet perfect among mornings.

Kino heard the creak of the rope when Juana took Coyotito out of his hanging box and cleaned him and hammocked him in her shawl in a loop that placed him close to her breast. Kino could see these things without looking at them. Juana sang softly an ancient song that had only three notes and yet endless variety of interval. And this was part of the family song too. It was all part. Sometimes it rose to an aching chord that caught the throat, saying this is safety, this is warmth, this is the *Whole*.

Across the brush fence were other brush houses, and the smoke came from them too, and the sound of breakfast, but those were other songs, their pigs were other pigs, their wives were not Juana. Kino was young and strong and his black hair hung over his brown forehead. His eyes were warm and fierce and bright and his moustache was thin and coarse. He lowered his blanket from his nose, for the dank poisonous air was gone and the yellow sunlight fell on the house. Near the brush fence two roosters bowed and feinted at each other with squared wings and neck feathers ruffed out. It would be a clumsy fight. They were not game chickens. Kino watched them for a moment, and then his eyes went up to a flight of wild doves twinkling inland to the hills. The world was awake now, and Kino arose and went into his brush house.

As he came through the door Juana stood up from the glowing fire pit. She put Coyotito back in his hanging box and then she combed her black hair and braided it in two braids and tied the ends with thin green ribbon. Kino squatted by the fire pit and rolled a hot corn-cake and dipped it in sauce and ate it. And he drank a little pulque and that was breakfast. That was the only breakfast he had ever known outside of feast days and one incredible fiesta on cookies that had nearly killed him. When Kino had finished, Juana came back to the fire and ate her breakfast. They had spoken once, but there is not need for speech if it is only a habit anyway. Kino sighed with satisfaction—and that was conversation.

The sun was warming the brush house, breaking through its crevices in long streaks. And one of the streaks fell on the hanging box where Coyotito lay, and on the ropes that held it.

9

It was a tiny movement that drew their eyes to the hanging box. Kino and Juana froze in their positions. Down the rope that hung the baby's box from the roof support a scorpion moved slowly. His stinging tail was straight out behind him, but he could whip it up in a flash of time.

Kino's breath whistled in his nostrils and he opened his mouth to stop it. And then the startled look was gone from him and the rigidity from his body. In his mind a new song had come, the Song of Evil, the music of the enemy, of any foe of the family, a savage, secret, dangerous melody, and underneath, the Song of the Family cried plaintively.

The scorpion moved delicately down the rope towards the box. Under her breath Juana repeated an ancient magic to guard against such evil, and on top of that she muttered a Hail Mary between clenched teeth. But Kino was in motion. His body glided quietly across the room, noiselessly and smoothly. His hands were in front of him, palms down, and his eyes were on the scorpion. Beneath it in the hanging box Coyotito laughed and reached up his hand towards it. It sensed danger when Kino was almost within reach of it. It stopped, and its tail rose up over its back in little jerks and the curved thorn on the tail's end glistened.

Kino stood perfectly still. He could hear Juana whispering the old magic again, and he could hear the evil music of the enemy. He could not move until the scorpion moved, and it felt for the source of the death that was coming to it. Kino's hand went forward very slowly, very smoothly. The thorned tail jerked upright. And at that moment the laughing Coyotito shook the rope and the scorpion fell.

Kino's hand leaped to catch it, but it fell past his fingers, fell on the baby's shoulder, landed and struck. Then, snarling, Kino had it, had it in his fingers, rubbing it to a paste in his hands. He threw it down and beat it into the earth floor with his fist, and Coyotito screamed with pain in his box. But Kino beat and stamped the enemy until it was only a fragment and a moist place in the dirt. His teeth were bared and fury flared in his eyes and the Song of the Enemy roared in his ears.

But Juana had the baby in her arms now. She found the puncture with redness starting from it already. She put her lips down over the puncture and sucked hard and spat and sucked again while Coyotito screamed.

Kino hovered; he was helpless, he was in the way.

The screams of the baby brought the neighbours. Out of their brush houses they poured—Kino's brother Juan Tomás and his fat wife Apolonia and their four children crowded in the door and blocked the entrance, while behind them others tried to look in, and one small boy crawled among legs to have a look. And those in front passed the word back to those behind—"Scorpion. The baby has been stung."

Juana stopped sucking the puncture for a moment. The little hole was slightly enlarged and its edges whitened from the sucking, but the red swelling extended farther around it in a hard lymphatic mound. And all of these people knew about the scorpion. An adult might be very ill from the sting, but a baby could easily die from the poison. First, they knew, would come swelling and fever and tightened throat, and then cramps in the stomach, and then Coyotito might die if enough of the poison had gone in. But the stinging pain of the bite was going away. Coyotito's screams turned to moans.

Kino had wondered often at the iron in his patient, fragile wife. She, who was obedient and respectful and cheerful and patient, could arch her back in child pain with hardly a cry. She could stand fatigue and hunger almost better than Kino himself. In the canoe she was like a strong man. And now she did a most surprising thing.

"The doctor," she said. "Go to get the doctor."

The word was passed out among the neighbours where they stood close-packed in the little yard behind the brush fence. And they repeated among themselves: "Juana wants the doctor." A wonderful thing, a memorable thing, to want the doctor. To get him would be a remarkable thing. The doctor never came to the cluster of brush houses. Why should he, when he had more than he could do to take care of the rich people who lived in the stone and plaster houses of the town?

"He would not come," the people in the yard said.

"He would not come," the people in the door said, and the thought got into Kino.

"The doctor would not come," Kino said to Juana.

She looked up at him, her eyes as cold as the eyes of a lioness. This was Juana's first baby—this was nearly everything there was in Juana's world. And Kino saw her determination and the music of the family sounded in his head with a steely tone.

"Then we will go to him," Juana said, and with one hand she arranged her dark-blue shawl over her head and made of one end of it a sling to hold the moaning baby and made of the other end of it a shade over his eyes to protect him from the light. The people in the door pushed against those behind to let her through. Kino followed her. They went out of the gate to the rutted path and the neighbours followed them.

The thing had become a neighbourhood affair. They made a quick soft-footed procession into the centre of the town, first Juana and Kino, and behind them Juan Tomás and Apolonia, her big stomach jiggling with the strenuous pace, then all the neighbours with the children trotting on the flanks. And the yellow sun threw their black shadows ahead of them so that they walked on their own shadows.

They came to the place where the brush houses stopped and the city of stone and plaster began, the city of harsh outer walls and inner cool gardens where a little water played and the bougainvillaea crusted the walls with purple and brick-red and white. They heard from the secret gardens the singing of caged birds and heard the splash of cooling water on hot flagstones. The procession crossed the blinding plaza and passed in front of the church. It had grown now, and in the outskirts the hurrying newcomers were being softly informed how the baby had been stung by a scorpion, how the father and mother were taking it to the doctor.

And the newcomers, particularly the beggars from the front of the church who were great experts in financial analysis, looked quickly at Juana's old blue skirt, saw the tears in her shawl, appraised the green ribbon on her braids, read the age of Kino's blanket and the thousand washings of his clothes, and set them down as poverty people and went along to see what kind of drama might develop. The four beggars in front of the church knew everything in the town. They were students of the expressions of young women as they went in to confession, and they saw them as they came out and read the nature of the sin. They knew every little scandal and some very big crimes. They slept at their posts in the shadow of the church so that no one crept in for consolation without their knowledge. And they knew the doctor. They knew his ignorance, his cruelty, his avarice, his appetites, his sins. They knew his clumsy abortions and the little brown pennies he gave sparingly for alms. They had seen his corpses go into the church. And, since early Mass was over and business was slow, they followed the procession, these endless searchers after perfect knowledge of their fellow men, to see what the fat lazy doctor would do about an indigent baby with a scorpion bite.

The scurrying procession came at last to the big gate in the wall of the doctor's house. They could hear the splashing of the water and the singing of caged birds and the sweep of the long brooms on the flagstones. And they could smell the frying of good bacon from the doctor's house.

Kino hesitated a moment. This doctor was not of his people. This doctor was of a race which for nearly four hundred years had beaten and starved and robbed and despised Kino's race, and frightened it too, so that the indigene came humbly to the door. And as always when he came near to one of this race, Kino felt weak and afraid and angry at the same time. Rage and terror went together. He could kill the doctor more easily than he could talk to him, for all of the doctor's race spoke to all of Kino's race as though they were simple animals. And as Kino raised his right hand to the iron ring knocker in the gate, rage swelled in him, and the pounding music of the enemy beat in his ears, and his lips drew tight against his teeth—but with his left hand he reached to take off his hat. The iron ring pounded against the gate. Kino took off his hat and stood waiting. Coyotito moaned a little in Juana's arms, and she spoke softly to him. The procession crowded close the better to see and hear.

After a moment the big gate opened a few inches. Kino could see the green coolness of the garden and little splashing fountain through the opening. The man who looked out at him was one of his own race. Kino spoke to him in the old language. "The little one—the first-born— has been poisoned by the scorpion," Kino said. "He requires the skill of the healer."

The gate closed a little, and the servant refused to speak in the old language. "A little moment," he said. "I go to inform myself," and he closed the gate and slid the bolt home. The glaring sun threw the bunched shadows of the people blackly on the white wall.

In his chamber the doctor sat up in his high bed. He had on his dressing-gown of red watered silk that had come from Paris, a little tight over the chest now if it was buttoned. On his lap was a silver tray with a silver chocolate pot and a tiny cup of egg-shell china, so delicate that it looked silly when he lifted it with his big hand, lifted it with the tips of thumb and forefinger and spread the other three fingers wide to get them out of the way. His eyes rested in puffy little hammocks of flesh and his mouth drooped with discontent. He was growing very stout, and his voice was hoarse with the fat that pressed on his throat. Beside him on a table was a small Oriental gong and a bowl of cigarettes. The furnishings of the room were heavy and dark and gloomy. The pictures were religious, even the large tinted photograph of his dead wife, who, if Masses willed and paid for out of her own estate could do it, was in Heaven. The doctor had once for a short time been a part of the great world and his whole subsequent life was memory and longing for France. "That," he said, "was civilized living"—by which he meant that on a small income he had been able to keep a mistress and eat in restaurants. He poured his second cup of chocolate and crumbled a sweet biscuit in his fingers. The servant from the gate came to the open door and stood waiting to be noticed.

"Yes?" the doctor asked.

"It is a little Indian with a baby. He says a scorpion stung it."

The doctor put his cup down gently before he let his anger rise.

"Have I nothing better to do than cure insect bites for 'little Indians'? I am a doctor, not a veterinary."

"Yes, Patron," said the servant.

"Has he any money?" the doctor demanded. "No, they never have any money. I, I alone in the world am supposed to work for nothing—and I am tired of it. See if he has any money!"

At the gate the servant opened the door a trifle and looked out at the waiting people. And this time he spoke in the old language.

"Have you money to pay for the treatment?"

Now Kino reached into a secret place somewhere under his blanket. He brought out a paper folded many times. Crease by crease he unfolded it, until at last there came to view eight small misshapen seed pearls, as ugly and grey as little ulcers, flattened and almost valueless. The servant took the paper and closed the gate again, but this time he was not gone long. He opened the gate just wide enough to pass the paper back.

"The doctor has gone out," he said. "He was called to a serious case." And he shut the gate quickly out of shame.

And now a wave of shame went over the whole procession. They melted away. The beggars went back to the church steps, the stragglers moved off, and the neighbours departed so that the public shaming of Kino would not be in their eyes.

For a long time Kino stood in front of the gate with Juana beside him. Slowly he put his suppliant hat on his head. Then, without warning, he struck the gate a crushing blow with his fist. He looked down in wonder at his split knuckles and at the blood that flowed down between his fingers.

II

THE town lay on a broad estuary, its old yellow plastered buildings hugging the beach. And on the beach the white and blue canoes that came from Nayarit were drawn up, canoes preserved for generations by a hard shell-like waterproof plaster whose making was a secret of the fishing people. They were high and graceful canoes with curving bow and stern and a braced section midships where a mast could be stepped to carry a small lateen sail.

The beach was yellow sand, but at the water's edge a rubble of shell and algae took its place. Fiddler crabs bubbled and sputtered in their holes in the sand, and in the shallows little lobsters popped in and out of their tiny homes in the rubble and sand. The sea bottom was rich with crawling and swimming and growing things. The brown algae waved in the gentle currents and the green eel grass swayed and little sea horses clung to its stems. Spotted botete, the poison fish, lay on the bottom in the eel-grass beds, and the bright-coloured swimming crabs scampered over them.

On the beach the hungry dogs and the hungry pigs of the town searched endlessly for any dead fish or sea bird that might have floated in on a rising tide.

Although the morning was young, the hazy mirage was

up. The uncertain air that magnified some things and blotted out others hung over the whole Gulf so that all sights were unreal and vision could not be trusted; so that sea and land had the sharp clarities and the vagueness of a dream. Thus it might be that the people of the Gulf trust things of the spirit and things of the imagination, but they do not trust their eyes to show them distance or clear outline or any optical exactness. Across the estuary from the town one section of mangroves stood clear and telescopically defined, while another mangrove clump was a hazy black-green blob. Part of the far shore disappeared into a shimmer that looked like water. There was no certainty in seeing, no proof that what you saw was there or was not there. And the people of the Gulf expected all places were that way, and it was not strange to them. A copper haze hung over the water, and the hot morning sun beat on it and made it vibrate blindingly.

The brush houses of the fishing people were back from the beach on the right-hand side of the town, and the canoes were drawn up in front of this area.

Kino and Juana came slowly down to the beach and to Kino's canoe, which was the one thing of value he owned in the world. It was very old. Kino's grandfather had brought it from Nayarit, and he had given it to Kino's father, and so it had come to Kino. It was at once property and source of food, for a man with a boat can guarantee a woman that she will eat something. It is the bulwark against starvation. And every year Kino refinished his canoe with the hard shell-like plaster by the secret method that had also come to him from his father. Now he came to the canoe and touched the bow tenderly as he always did. He laid his diving-rock and his basket and the two ropes in the sand by the canoe. And he folded his blanket and laid it in the bow.

Juana laid Coyotito on the blanket, and she placed her shawl over him so that the hot sun could not shine on him. He was quiet now, but the swelling on his shoulder had continued up his neck and under his ear and his face was puffed and feverish. Juana went to the water and waded in. She gathered some brown seaweed and made a flat damp poultice of it, and this she applied to the baby's swollen shoulder, which was as good a remedy as any and probably better than the doctor could have done. But the remedy lacked his authority because it was simple and didn't cost anything. The stomach cramps had not come to Coyotito. Perhaps Juana had sucked out the poison in time, but she had not sucked out her worry over her first-born. She had not prayed directly for the recovery of the baby—she had prayed that they might find a pearl with which to hire the doctor to cure the baby, for the minds of people are as unsubstantial as the mirage of the Gulf.

Now Kino and Juana slid the canoe down the beach to the water, and when the bow floated, Juana climbed in, while Kino pushed the stern in and waded beside it until it floated lightly and trembled on the little breaking waves. Then in co-ordination Juana and Kino drove their double-bladed paddles into the sea, and the canoe creased the water and hissed with speed. The other pearlers were gone out long since. In a few moments Kino could see them clustered in the haze, riding over the oyster bed.

Light filtered down through the water to the bed where the frilly pearl oysters lay fastened to the rubbly bottom, a bottom strewn with shells of broken, opened oysters. This was the bed that had raised the King of Spain to be a great power in Europe in past years, had helped to pay for his wars, and had decorated the churches for his soul's sake. The grey oysters with ruffles like skirts on the shells, the barnacle-crusted oysters with little bits of weed cling-ing to the skirts and small crabs climbing over them. An accident could happen to these oysters, a grain of sand could lie in the folds of muscle and irritate the flesh until in self-protection the flesh coated the grain with a layer of smooth cement. But once started, the flesh continued to coat the foreign body until it fell free in some tidal flurry or until the oyster was destroyed. For centuries men had dived down and torn the oysters from the beds and ripped them open, looking for the coated grains of sand. Swarms of fish lived near the bed to live near the oysters thrown back by the searching men and to nibble at the shining inner shells. But the pearls were accidents, and the finding of one was luck, a little pat on the back by God or the gods or both.

Kino had two ropes, one tied to a heavy stone and one to a basket. He stripped off his shirt and trousers and laid his hat in the bottom of the canoe. The water was oily smooth. He took his rock in one hand and his basket in the other, and he slipped feet first over the side and the rock carried him to the bottom. The bubbles rose behind him until the water cleared and he could see. Above, the surface of the water was an undulating mirror of brightness, and he could see the bottoms of the canoes sticking through it.

Kino moved cautiously so that the water would not be obscured with mud or sand. He hooked his foot in the loop on his rock and his hands worked quickly, tearing the oysters loose, some singly, others in clusters. He laid them in his basket. In some places the oysters clung to one another so that they came free in lumps.

Now Kino's people had sung of everything that happened or existed. They had made songs to the fishes, to the sea in anger and to the sea in calm, to the light and the dark and the sun and the moon, and the songs were all in Kino and in his people—every song that had ever been made, even the ones forgotten. And as he filled his basket the song was in Kino, and the beat of the song was his pounding heart as it ate the oxygen from his held breath, and the melody of the song was the grey-green water and the little scuttling animals and the clouds of fish that flitted by and were gone. But in the song there was a secret little inner song, hardly perceptible, but always there, sweet and secret and clinging, almost hiding in the counter-melody, and this was the Song of the Pearl That Might Be, for every shell thrown in the basket might contain a pearl. Chance was against it, but luck and the gods

19

might be for it. And in the canoe above him Kino knew that Juana was making the magic of prayer, her face set rigid and her muscles hard to force the luck, to tear the luck out of the gods' hands, for she needed the luck for the swollen shoulder of Coyotito. And because the need was great and the desire was great, the little secret melody of the pearl that might be was stronger this morning. Whole phrases of it came clearly and softly into the Song of the Undersea.

Kino, in his pride and youth and strength, could remain down over two minutes without strain, so that he worked deliberately, selecting the largest shells. Because they were disturbed, the oyster shells were tightly closed. A little to his right a hummock of rubbly rock struck up, covered with young oysters not ready to take. Kino moved next to the hummock, and then, beside it, under a little over-hang, he saw a very large oyster lying by itself, not covered with its clinging brothers. The shell was partly open, for the overhang protected this ancient oyster, and in the lip-like muscle Kino saw a ghostly gleam, and then the shell closed down. His heart beat out a heavy rhythm and the melody of the maybe pearl shrilled in his ears. Slowly he forced the oyster loose and held it tightly against his breast. He kicked his foot free from the rock loop, and his body rose to the surface and his black hair gleamed in the sunlight. He reached over the side of the canoe and laid the oyster in the bottom.

Then Juana steadied the boat while he climbed in. His eyes were shining with excitement, but in decency he pulled up his rock, and then he pulled up his basket of oysters and lifted them in. Juana sensed his excitement, and she pretended to look away. It is not good to want a thing too much. It sometimes drives the luck away. You must want it just enough, and you must be very tactful with God or the gods. But Juana stopped breathing. Very deliberately Kino opened his short strong knife. He looked speculatively at the basket. Perhaps it would be better to open *the* oyster last. He took a small oyster from the basket, cut the muscle, searched the folds of flesh, and threw it in the water. Then he seemed to see the great oyster for the first time. He squatted in the bottom of the canoe, picked up the shell and examined it. The flutes were shining black to brown, and only a few small barnacles adhered to the shell. Now Kino was reluctant to open it. What he had seen, he knew, might be a reflection, a piece of flat shell accidentally drifted in or a complete illusion. In this Gulf of uncertain light there were more illusions than realities.

But Juana's eyes were on him and she could not wait. She put her hand on Coyotito's covered head. "Open it," she said softly.

Kino deftly slipped his knife into the edge of the shell. Through the knife he could feel the muscle tighten hard. He worked the blade lever-wise and the closing muscle parted and the shell fell apart. The lip-like flesh writhed up and then subsided. Kino lifted the flesh, and there it lay, the great pearl, perfect as the moon. It captured the light and refined it and gave it back in silver incandescence. It was as large as a seagull's egg. It was the greatest pearl in the world.

Juana caught her breath and moaned a little. And to Kino the secret melody of the maybe pearl broke clear and beautiful, rich and warm and lovely, glowing and gloating and triumphant. In the surface of the great pearl he could see dream forms. He picked the pearl from the dying flesh and held it in his palm, and he turned it over and saw that its curve was perfect. Juana came near to stare at it in his hand, and it was the hand he had smashed against the doctor's gate, and the torn flesh of the knuckles was turned greyish-white by the sea-water.

Instinctively Juana went to Coyotito where he lay on his father's blanket. She lifted the poultice of sea-weed and looked at the shoulder. "Kino," she cried shrilly.

He looked past his pearl, and he saw that the swelling was going out of the baby's shoulder, the poison was receding from its body. Then Kino's fist closed over the pearl and his emotion broke over him. He put back his head and howled. His eyes rolled up and he screamed and his body was rigid. The men in the other canoes looked up, startled, and then they dug their paddles into the sea and raced towards Kino's canoe.

<h1 style="text-align:center">I I I</h1>

A TOWN is a thing like a colonial animal. A town has a nervous system and a head and shoulders and feet. A town is a thing separate from all other towns, so that there are no two towns alike. And a town has a whole emotion. How news travels through a town is a mystery not easily to be solved. News seems to move faster than small boys can scramble and dart to tell it, faster than women can call it over the fences.

Before Kino and Juana and the other fishers had come to Kino's brush house, the nerves of the town were pulsing and vibrating with the news—Kino had found the Pearl of the World. Before panting little boys could strangle out the words, their mothers knew it. The news swept on past the brush houses, and it washed in a foaming wave into the town of stone and plaster. It came to the priest walking in his garden, and it put a thoughtful look in his eyes and a memory of certain repairs necessary to the church. He wondered what the pearl would be worth. And he wondered whether he had baptized Kino's baby, or married him for that matter. The news came to the shopkeepers, and they looked at men's clothes that had not sold so well.

The news came to the doctor where he sat with a woman whose illness was age, though neither she nor the doctor would admit it. And when it was made plain who Kino was, the doctor grew stern and judicious at the same time. "He is a client of mine," the doctor said. "I am treating his child for a scorpion sting." And the doctor's eyes rolled up a little in their fat hammocks and he thought of Paris. He remembered the room he had lived in there as a great and luxurious place, and he remembered the hard-faced woman who had lived with him as a beautiful and kind girl, although she had been none of these three. The doctor looked past his aged patient and saw himself sitting in a restaurant in Paris and a waiter was just opening a bottle of wine.

The news came early to the beggars in front of the church, and it made them giggle a little with pleasure, for they knew that there is no alms-giver in the world like a poor man who is suddenly lucky.

Kino had found the Pearl of the World. In the town, in little offices, sat the men who bought pearls from the fishers. They waited in their chairs until the pearls came in and then they cackled and fought and shouted and threatened until they reached the lowest price the fishermen would stand. But there was a price below which they dared not go, for it had happened that a fisherman in despair had given his pearls to the church. And when the buying was over, these buyers sat alone and their fingers played restlessly with the pearls, and they wished they owned the pearls. For there were not many buyers really —there was only one, and he kept these agents in separate offices to give a semblance of competition. The news came to these men, and their eyes squinted and their finger-tips burned a little, and each one thought how the patron could not live forever and someone had to take his place. And each one thought how with some capital he could get a new start.

All manner of people grew interested in Kino—people with things to sell and people with favours to ask. Kino had found the Pearl of the World. The essence of pearl mixed with essence of men and a curious dark residue was precipitated. Every man suddenly became related to Kino's pearl, and Kino's pearl went into the dreams, the speculations, the schemes, the plans, the futures, the wishes, the needs, the lusts, the hungers, of everyone, and only one person stood in the way and that was Kino, so that he became curiously every man's enemy. The news stirred up something infinitely black and evil in the town; the black distillate was like the scorpion, or like hunger in the smell of food, or like loneliness when love is withheld. The poison sacs of the town began to manufacture venom, and the town swelled and puffed with the pressure of it.

But Kino and Juana did not know these things. Because they were happy and excited they thought everyone shared their joy. Juan Tomás and Apolonia did, and they were the world too. In the afternoon, when the sun had gone over the mountains of the Peninsula to sink in the outward sea, Kino squatted in his house with Juana beside him. And the brush house was crowded with neighbours. Kino held the great pearl in his hand, and it was warm and alive in his hand. And the music of the pearl had merged with the music of the family so that one beautified the other. The neighbours looked at the pearl in Kino's hand and they wondered how such luck could come to any man.

And Juan Tomás, who squatted on Kino's right hand because he was his brother, asked: "What will you do now that you have become a rich man?"

Kino looked into his pearl, and Juana cast her eyelashes down and arranged her shawl to cover her face so that her excitement could not be seen. And in the incandescence of the pearl the pictures formed of the things Kino's mind had considered in the past and had given up as impossible. In the pearl he saw Juana and Coyotito and himself standing and kneeling at the high altar, and they were being married now that they could pay. He spoke softly: "We will be married—in the church."

In the pearl he saw how they were dressed—Juana in a shawl stiff with newness and a new skirt, and from under the long skirt Kino could see that she wore shoes. It was in the pearl—the picture glowing there. He himself was dressed in new white clothes, and he carried a new hat—not of straw but of fine black felt—and he too wore shoes

24

—not sandals but shoes that laced. But Coyotito—he was the one—he wore a blue sailor suit from the United States and a little yachting cap such as Kino had seen once when a pleasure-boat put into the estuary. All of these things Kino saw in the lucent pearl, and he said : "We will have new clothes."

And the music of the pearl rose like a chorus of trumpets in his ears.

Then to the lovely grey surface of the pearl came the little things Kino wanted : a harpoon to take the place of one lost a year ago, a new harpoon of iron with a ring in the end of the shaft; and—his mind could hardly make the leap—a rifle—but why not, since he was so rich? And Kino saw Kino in the pearl, Kino holding a Winchester carbine. It was the wildest day-dreaming and very pleasant. His lips moved hesitantly over this. "A rifle," he said. "Perhaps a rifle."

It was the rifle that broke down the barriers. This was an impossibility, and if he could think of having a rifle whole horizons were burst and he could rush on. For it is said that humans are never satisfied, that you give them one thing and they want something more. And this is said in disparagement, whereas it is one of the greatest talents the species has and one that has made it superior to animals that are satisfied with what they have.

The neighbours, close pressed and silent in the house, nodded their heads at his wild imaginings. And a man in the rear murmured : "A rifle. He will have a rifle."

But the music of the pearl was shrilling with triumph in Kino. Juana looked up, and her eyes were wide at Kino's courage and at his imagination. And electric strength had come to him now the horizons were kicked out. In the pearl he saw Coyotito sitting at a little desk in a school, just as Kino had once seen it through an open door. And Coyotito was dressed in a jacket, and he had on a white collar and a broad silken tie. Moreover, Coyotito was writing on a big piece of paper. Kino looked at his neighbours fiercely. "My son will go to school," he said, and the neighbours were hushed. Juana caught her breath sharply. Her eyes were bright as she watched him, and she looked quickly down at Coyotito in her arms to see whether this might be possible.

But Kino's face shone with prophecy. "My son will read and open the books, and my son will write and will know writing. And my son will make numbers, and these things will make us free because he will know—he will know and through him we will know." And in the pearl Kino saw himself and Juana squatting by the little fire in the brush hut while Coyotito read from a great book. "This is what the pearl will do," said Kino. And he had never said so many words together in his life. And suddenly he was afraid of his talking. His hand closed down over the pearl and cut the light away from it. Kino was afraid as a man is afraid who says: "I will," without knowing.

Now the neighbours knew they had witnessed a great marvel. They knew that time would now date from Kino's pearl, and that they would discuss this moment for many years to come. If these things came to pass, they would recount how Kino looked and what he said and how his eyes shone, and they would say: "He was a man transfigured. Some power was given to him, and there it started. You see what a great man he has become, starting from that moment. And I myself saw it."

And if Kino's planning came to nothing, those same neighbours would say: "There it started. A foolish madness came over him so that he spoke foolish words. God keep us from such things. Yes, God punished Kino because he rebelled against the way things are. You see what has become of him. And I myself saw the moment when his reason left him."

Kino looked down at his closed hand and the knuckles were scabbed over and tight where he had struck the gate.

Now the dusk was coming. And Juana looped her shawl under the baby so that he hung against her hip, and she went to the fire hole and dug a coal from the ashes and broke a few twigs over it and fanned a flame alive. The little flames danced on the faces of the neighbours. They knew they should go to their own dinners, but they were reluctant to leave.

The dark was almost in, and Juana's fire threw shadows on the brush walls when the whisper came in, passed from mouth to mouth. "The Father is coming—the priest is coming." Then men uncovered their heads and stepped back from the door, and the women gathered their shawls about their faces and cast down their eyes. Kino and Juan Tomás, his brother, stood up. The priest came in— a greying, ageing man with an old skin and a young sharp eye. Children he considered these people, and he treated them like children.

"Kino," he said softly, "thou art named after a great man—and a great Father of the Church." He made it sound like a benediction. "Thy namesake tamed the desert and sweetened the minds of thy people, didst thou know that? It is in the books."

Kino looked quickly down at Coyotito's head, where he hung on Juana's hip. Some day, his mind said, that boy would know what things were in the books and what things were not. The music had gone out of Kino's head, but now, thinly, slowly, the melody of the morning, the music of evil, of the enemy, sounded, but it was faint and weak. And Kino looked at his neighbours to see who might have brought this song in.

But the priest was speaking again. "It has come to me that thou hast found a great fortune, a great pearl."

Kino opened his hand and held it out, and the priest gasped a little at the size and beauty of the pearl. And then he said : "I hope thou wilt remember to give thanks, my son, to Him who has given thee this treasure, and to pray for guidance in the future."

Kino nodded dumbly, and it was Juana who spoke softly. "We will, Father. And we will be married now. Kino has said so." She looked at the neighbours for confirmation, and they nodded their heads solemnly.

The priest said: "It is pleasant to see that your first thoughts are good thoughts. God bless you, my children." He turned and left quietly, and the people let him through.

But Kino's hand had closed tightly on the pearl again, and he was glancing about suspiciously, for the evil song was in his ears, shrilling against the music of the pearl.

The neighbours slipped away to go to their houses, and Juana squatted by the fire and set her clay pot of boiled beans over the little flame. Kino stepped to the doorway and looked out. As always, he could smell the smoke from many fires, and he could see the hazy stars and feel the damp of the night air so that he covered his nose from it. The thin dog came to him and threshed itself in greeting like a wind-blown flag, and Kino looked down at it and didn't see it. He had broken through the horizons into a cold and lonely outside. He felt alone and unprotected, and scraping crickets and shrilling tree frogs and croaking toads seemed to be carrying the melody of evil. Kino shivered a little and drew his blanket more tightly against his nose. He carried the pearl still in his hand, tightly closed in his palm, and it was warm and smooth against his skin.

Behind him he heard Juana patting the cakes before she put them down on the clay cooking-sheet. Kino felt all the warmth and security of his family behind him, and the Song of the Family came from behind him like the purring of a kitten. But now, by saying what his future was going to be like, he had created it. A plan is a real thing, and things projected are experienced. A plan once made and visualized becomes a reality along with other realities—never to be destroyed but easily to be attacked. Thus Kino's future was real, but having set it up, other forces were set up to destroy it, and this he knew, so that he had to prepare to meet the attack. And this Kino knew also—that the gods do not love men's plans, and the gods do not love success unless it comes by accident. He knew that the gods take their revenge on a man if he be successful through his own efforts. Consequently Kino was afraid of plans, but having made one, he could never destroy it. And to meet the attack, Kino was already making a hard skin for himself against the world. His eyes and his mind probed for danger before it appeared.

Standing in the door, he saw two men approach; and one of them carried a lantern which lighted the ground and the legs of the men. They turned in through the opening of Kino's brush fence and came to his door. And Kino saw that one was the doctor and the other the servant who had opened the gate in the morning. The split knuckles on Kino's right hand burned when he saw who they were.

The doctor said : "I was not in when you came this morning. But now, at the first chance, I have come to see the baby."

Kino stood in the door, filling it, and hatred raged and flamed in the back of his eyes, and fear too, for the hundreds of years of subjugation were cut deep in him.

"The baby is nearly well now," he said curtly.

The doctor smiled, but his eyes in their little lymph-lined hammocks did not smile.

He said : "Sometimes, my friend, the scorpion sting has a curious effect. There will be apparent improvement, and then without warning—pouf !" He pursed his lips and made a little explosion to show how quick it could be, and he shifted his small black doctor's bag about so that the light of the lamp fell upon it, for he knew that Kino's race love the tools of any craft and trust them. "Sometimes," the doctor went on in a liquid tone, "sometimes there will be a withered leg or a blind eye or a crumpled back. Oh, I know the sting of the scorpion, my friend, and I can cure it."

Kino felt the rage and hatred melting towards fear. He did not know, and perhaps this doctor did. And he could not take the chance of putting his certain ignorance against this man's possible knowledge. He was trapped as his people were always trapped, and would be until, as he had said, they could be sure that the things in the books were really in the books. He could not take a chance—not with the life or with the straightness of Coyotito. He stood aside and let the doctor and his man enter the brush hut.

Juana stood up from the fire and backed away as he entered, and she covered the baby's face with the fringe of her shawl. And when the doctor went to her and held out his hand, she clutched the baby tight and looked at Kino where he stood with the fire shadows leaping on his face.

Kino nodded, and only then did she let the doctor take the baby.

"Hold the light," the doctor said, and when the servant held the lantern high, the doctor looked for a moment at the wound on the baby's shoulder. He was thoughtful for a moment and then he rolled back the baby's eyelid and looked at the eyeball. He nodded his head while Coyotito struggled against him.

"It is as I thought," he said. "The poison has gone inwards and it will strike soon. Come, look!" He held the eyelid down. "See—it is blue." And Kino, looking anxiously, saw that indeed it was a little blue. And he didn't know whether or not it was always blue. But the trap was set. He couldn't take the chance.

The doctor's eyes watered in their little hammocks. "I will give him something to try to turn the poison aside," he said. And he handed the baby to Kino.

Then from his bag he took a little bottle of white powder and a capsule of gelatine. He filled the capsule with the powder and closed it, and then around the first capsule he fitted a second capsule and closed it. Then he worked very deftly. He took the baby and pinched its lower lip until it opened its mouth. His fat fingers placed the capsule far back on the baby's tongue, back of the point where he could spit it out, and then from the floor he picked up the little pitcher of pulque and gave Coyotito a drink, and it was done. He looked again at the baby's eyeballs and he pursed his lips and seemed to think.

At last he handed the baby back to Juana, and he turned to Kino. "I think the poison will attack within the hour," he said. "The medicine may save the baby from hurt, but I will come back in an hour. Perhaps I am in time to save him." He took a deep breath and went out of the hut, and his servant followed him with the lantern.

Now Juana had the baby under the shawl, and she stared at it with anxiety and fear. Kino came to her, and he lifted the shawl and stared at the baby. He moved his hand to look under the eyelid, and only then saw that the pearl was still in his hand. Then he went to a box by the wall, and from it he brought a piece of rag. He wrapped the pearl in the rag, then went to the corner of the brush house and dug a little hole with his fingers in the dirt floor, and he put the pearl in the hole and covered it up and concealed the place. And then he went to the fire where Juana was squatting, watching the baby's face.

The doctor, back in his house, settled into his chair and looked at his watch. His people brought him a little supper of chocolate and sweet cakes and fruit, and he stared at the food discontentedly.

In the houses of the neighbours the subject that would lead all conversations for a long time to come was aired for the first time to see how it would go. The neighbours showed one another with their thumbs how big the pearl was, and they made little caressing gestures to show how lovely it was. From now on they would watch Kino and Juana very closely to see whether riches turned their heads, as riches turn all people's heads. Everyone knew why the doctor had come. He was not good at dissembling and he was very well understood.

Out in the estuary a tight woven school of small fishes glittered and broke water to escape a school of great fishes that drove in to eat them. And in the houses the people could hear the swish of the small ones and the bouncing splash of the great ones as the slaughter went on. The dampness arose out of the Gulf and was deposited on the bushes and cacti and on little trees in salty drops. And the night mice crept about on the ground and the little night hawks hunted them silently.

The skinny black puppy with flame spots over his eyes came to Kino's door and looked in. He nearly shook his hindquarters loose when Kino glanced up at him, and he subsided when Kino looked away. The puppy did not enter the house, but he watched with frantic interest while Kino ate his beans from the little pottery dish and wiped it clean with a corn-cake and ate the cake and washed the whole down with a drink of pulque.

Kino was finished and was rolling a cigarette when Juana spoke sharply. "Kino." He glanced at her and then got up and went quickly to her for he saw fright in her eyes. He stood over her, looking down, but the light was very dim. He kicked a pile of twigs into the fire hole to make a blaze, and then he could see the face of Coyotito. The baby's face was flushed and his throat was working and a little thick drool of saliva issued from his lips. The spasm of the stomach muscles began, and the baby was very sick.

Kino knelt beside his wife. "So the doctor knew," he said, but he said it for himself as well as for his wife, for his mind was hard and suspicious and he was remembering the white powder. Juana rocked from side to side and moaned out the little Song of the Family as though it could ward off the danger, and the baby vomited and writhed in her arms. Now uncertainty was in Kino, and the music of evil throbbed in his head and nearly drove out Juana's song.

The doctor finished his chocolate and nibbled the little fallen pieces of sweet cake. He brushed his fingers on a napkin, looked at his watch, arose, and took up his little bag.

The news of the baby's illness travelled quickly among the brush houses, for sickness is second only to hunger as the enemy of poor people. And some said softly : "Luck, you see, brings bitter friends." And they nodded and got up to go to Kino's house. The neighbours scuttled with covered noses through the dark until they crowded into Kino's house again. They stood and gazed, and they made little comments on the sadness that this should happen at a time of joy, and they said : "All things are in God's hands." The old women squatted down beside Juana to try to give her aid if they could and comfort if they could not.

Then the doctor hurried in, followed by his man. He scattered the old women like chickens. He took the baby and examined it and felt its head. "The poison it has worked," he said. "I think I can defeat it. I will try my best." He asked for water, and in the cup of it he put three drops of ammonia, and he pried open the baby's mouth and poured it down. The baby spluttered and screeched under the treatment, and Juana watched him with haunted eyes. The doctor spoke a little as he worked. "It is lucky that I know about the poison of the scorpion, otherwise——" And he shrugged to show what could have happened.

But Kino was suspicious, and he could not take his eyes from the doctor's open bag, and from the bottle of white powder there. Gradually the spasms subsided and the baby relaxed under the doctor's hands. And then Coyotito sighed deeply and went to sleep, for he was very tired with vomiting.

The doctor put the baby in Juana's arms. "He will get well now," he said. "I have won the fight." And Juana looked at him with adoration.

The doctor was closing his bag now. He said : "When do you think you can pay this bill?" He said it even kindly.

"When I have sold my pearl I will pay you," Kino said.

"You have a pearl? A good pearl?" the doctor asked with interest.

And then the chorus of the neighbours broke in. "He has found the Pearl of the World," they cried, and they joined forefinger with thumb to show how great the pearl was.

"Kino will be a rich man," they clamoured. "It is a pearl such as one has never seen."

The doctor looked surprised. "I had not heard of it. Do you keep this pearl in a safe place? Perhaps you would like me to put it in my safe?"

Kino's eyes were hooded now, his cheeks were drawn taut. "I have it secure," he said. "Tomorrow I will sell it and then I will pay you."

The doctor shrugged, and his wet eyes never left Kino's eyes. He knew the pearl would be buried in the house, and he thought Kino might look towards the place where it was buried. "It would be a shame to have it stolen before you could sell it," the doctor said, and he saw Kino's eyes flick involuntarily to the floor near the side post of the brush house.

When the doctor had gone and all the neighbours had reluctantly returned to their houses, Kino squatted beside the little glowing coals in the fire hole and listened to the night sound, the soft sweep of the little waves on the shore and the distant barking of dogs, the creeping of the breeze through the brush-house roof and the soft speech of his neighbours in their houses in the village. For these people do not sleep soundly all night; they awaken at intervals and talk a little and then go to sleep again. And after a while Kino got up and went to the door of his house.

He smelled the breeze and he listened for any foreign sound of secrecy or creeping, and his eyes searched the darkness, for the music of evil was sounding in his head and he was fierce and afraid. After he had probed the night with his senses he went to the place by the side post where the pearl was buried, and he dug it up and brought it to his sleeping-mat, and under his sleeping-mat he dug another little hole in the dirt floor and buried his pearl and covered it up again.

And Juana, sitting by the fire hole, watched him with questioning eyes, and when he had buried his pearl she asked : "Who do you fear?"

34

Kino searched for a true answer, and at last he said : "Everyone." And he could feel a shell of hardness drawing over him.

After a while they lay down together on the sleeping-mat, and Juana did not put the baby in his box tonight, but cradled him on her arms and covered his face with her head-shawl. And the last light went out of the embers in the fire hole.

But Kino's brain burned, even during his sleep, and he dreamed that Coyotito could read, that one of his own people could tell the truth of things. And in his dream, Coyotito was reading from a book as large as a house, with letters as big as dogs, and the words galloped and played on the book. And then darkness spread over the page, and with the darkness came the music of evil again, and Kino stirred in his sleep; and when he stirred, Juana's eyes opened in the darkness. And then Kino awakened, with the evil music pulsing in him, and he lay in the darkness with his ears alert.

Then from the corner of the house came a sound so soft that it might have been simply a thought, a little furtive movement, a touch of a foot on earth, the almost inaudible purr of controlled breathing. Kino held his breath to listen, and he knew that whatever dark thing was in his house was holding its breath too, to listen. For a time no sound at all came from the corner of the brush house. Then Kino might have thought he had imagined the sound. But Juana's hand came creeping over to him in warning, and then the sound came again : the whisper of a foot on dry earth and the scratch of fingers in the soil.

And now a wild fear surged in Kino's breast, and on the fear came rage, as it always did. Kino's hand crept into his breast where his knife hung on a string, and then he sprang like an angry cat, leaped striking and spitting for the dark thing he knew was in the corner of the house. He felt cloth, struck at it with his knife and missed, and struck again and felt his knife go through cloth, and then his head crashed with lightning and exploded with pain.

35

There was a soft scurry in the doorway, and running steps for a moment, and then silence.

Kino could feel warm blood running down from his forehead, and he could hear Juana calling to him. "Kino! Kino!" And there was terror in her voice. Then coldness came over him as quickly as the rage had, and he said: "I am all right. The thing has gone."

He groped his way back to the sleeping-mat. Already Juana was working at the fire. She uncovered an ember from the ashes and shredded little pieces of corn-husk over it and blew a little flame into the corn-husks so that a tiny light danced through the hut. And then from a secret place Juana brought a little piece of consecrated candle and lighted it at the flame and set it upright on a fireplace stone. She worked quickly, crooning as she moved about. She dipped the end of her head-shawl in water and swabbed the blood from Kino's bruised forehead. "It is nothing," Kino said, but his eyes and his voice were hard and cold and a brooding hate was growing in him.

Now the tension which had been growing in Juana boiled up to the surface and her lips were thin. "This thing is evil," she cried harshly. "This pearl is like a sin! It will destroy us," and her voice rose shrilly. "Throw it away, Kino. Let us break it between stones. Let us bury it and forget the place. Let us throw it back into the sea. It has brought evil. Kino, my husband, it will destroy us." And in the firelight her lips and her eyes were alive with her fear.

But Kino's face was set, and his mind and his will were set. "This is our one chance," he said. "Our son must go to school. He must break out of the pot that holds us in."

"It will destroy us all," Juana cried. "Even our son."

"Hush," said Kino. "Do not speak any more. In the morning we will sell the pearl, and then the evil will be gone, and only the good remain. Now hush, my wife." His dark eyes scowled into the little fire, and for the first time he knew that his knife was still in his hands, and he

36

raised the blade and looked at it and saw a little line of blood on the steel. For a moment he seemed about to wipe the blade on his trousers, but then he plunged the knife into the earth and so cleansed it.

The distant roosters began to crow and the air changed and the dawn was coming. The wind of the morning ruffled the water of the estuary and whispered through the mangroves, and the little waves beat on the rubbly beach with an increased tempo. Kino raised the sleeping-mat and dug up his pearl and put it in front of him and stared at it.

And the beauty of the pearl, winking and glimmering in the little candle, cozened his brain with its beauty. So lovely it was, so soft, and its own music came from it—its music of promise and delight, its guarantee of the future, of comfort, of security. Its warm lucence promised a poultice against illness and a wall against insult. It closed a door on hunger. And as he stared at it Kino's eyes softened and his face relaxed. He could see the little image of the consecrated candle reflected in the soft surface of the pearl, and he heard again in his ears the lovely music of the undersea, the tone of the diffused green light of the sea bottom. Juana, glancing secretly at him, saw him smile. And because they were in some way one thing and one purpose, she smiled with him.

And they began this day with hope.

IV

IT is wonderful the way a little town keeps track of itself and of all its units. If every single man and woman, child and baby, acts and conducts itself in a known pattern and breaks no walls and differs with no one and experiments in no way and is not sick and does not endanger the ease and peace of mind or steady unbroken flow of the town, then that unit can disappear and never be heard of. But

37

let one man step out of the regular thought or the known and trusted pattern, and the nerves of the townspeople ring with nervousness and communication travels over the nerve lines of the town. Then every unit communicates to the whole.

Thus, in La Paz, it was known in the early morning through the whole town that Kino was going to sell his pearl that day. It was known among the neighbours in the brush huts, among the pearl fishermen; it was known among the Chinese grocery-store owners; it was known in the church, for the altar boys whispered about it. Word of it crept in among the nuns; the beggars in front of the church spoke of it, for they would be there to take the tithe of the first fruits of the luck. The little boys knew about it with excitement, but most of all the pearl buyers knew about it, and when the day had come, in the offices of the pearl buyers, each man sat alone with his little black velvet tray, and each man rolled the pearls about with his finger-tips and considered his part in the picture.

It was supposed that the pearl buyers were individuals acting alone, bidding against one another for the pearls the fishermen brought in. And once it had been so. But this was a wasteful method, for often, in the excitement of bidding for a fine pearl, too great a price had been paid to the fishermen. This was extravagant and not to be countenanced. Now there was only one pearl buyer with many hands, and the men who sat in their offices and waited for Kino knew what price they would offer, how high they would bid, and what method each one would use. And although these men would not profit beyond their salaries, there was excitement among the pearl buyers, for there was excitement in the hunt, and if it be a man's function to break down a price, then he must take joy and satisfaction in breaking it as far down as possible. For every man in the world functions to the best of his ability, and no one does less than his best, no matter what he may think about it. Quite apart from any reward they might get, from any word of praise, from any promotion, a pearl buyer was a pearl buyer, and the best and happiest pearl buyer was he who bought for the lowest prices.

The sun was hot yellow that morning, and it drew the moisture from the estuary and from the Gulf and hung it in shimmering scarves in the air so that the air vibrated and vision was unsubstantial. A vision hung in the air to the north of the city—the vision of a mountain that was over two hundred miles away, and the high slopes of this mountain were swaddled with pines and a great stone peak arose above the timber line.

And the morning of this day the canoes lay lined up on the beach; the fishermen did not go out to dive for pearls, for there would be too much happening, too many things to see when Kino went to sell the great pearl.

In the brush houses by the shore Kino's neighbours sat long over their breakfasts, and they spoke of what they would do if they had found the pearl. And one man said he would give it as a present to the Holy Father in Rome. Another said that he would buy Masses for the souls of his family for a thousand years. Another thought he might take the money and distribute it among the poor of La Paz; and a fourth thought of all the good things one could do with the money from the pearl, of all the charities, benefits, of all the rescues one could perform if one had money. All of the neighbours hoped that sudden wealth would not turn Kino's head, would not make a rich man of him, would not graft on to him the evil limbs of greed and hatred and coldness. For Kino was a well-liked man; it would be a shame if the pearl destroyed him. "That good wife Juana," they said, "and the beautiful baby Coyotito, and the others to come. What a pity it would be if the pearl should destroy them all."

For Kino and Juana this was the morning of mornings of their lives, comparable only to the day when the baby had been born. This was to be the day from which all other days would take their arrangement. Thus they would say : "It was two years before we sold the pearl," or, "It was six weeks after we sold the pearl." Juana, considering the matter, threw caution to the winds, and she dressed Coyotito in the clothes she had prepared for his baptism, when there would be money for his baptism. And Juana combed and braided her hair and tied the ends with two little bows of red ribbon, and she put on her marriage skirt and waist. The sun was quarter high when they were ready. Kino's ragged white clothes were clean at least, and this was the last day of his raggedness. For tomorrow, or even this afternoon, he would have new clothes.

The neighbours, watching Kino's door through the crevices in their brush houses, were dressed and ready too. There was no self-consciousness about their joining Kino and Juana to go pearl selling. It was expected, it was an historic moment, they would be crazy if they didn't go. It would be almost a sign of unfriendship.

Juana put on her head-shawl carefully, and she draped one long end under her right elbow and gathered it with her right hand so that a hammock hung under her arm, and in this little hammock she placed Coyotito, propped up against the head shawl so that he could see everything and perhaps remember. Kino put on his large straw hat and felt it with his hand to see that it was properly placed, not on the back or side of his head, like a rash, unmarried, irresponsible man, and not flat as an elder would wear it, but lifted a little forward to show aggressiveness and seriousness and vigour. There is a great deal to be seen in the tilt of a hat on a man. Kino slipped his feet into his sandals and pulled the thongs up over his heels. The great pearl was wrapped in an old soft piece of deerskin and placed in a little leather bag, and the leather bag was in a pocket in Kino's shirt. He folded his blanket carefully and draped it in a narrow strip over his left shoulder, and now they were ready.

Kino stepped with dignity out of the house, and Juana followed him, carrying Coyotito. And as they marched up the freshet-washed alley towards the town, the neighbours joined them. The houses belched people; the doorways spewed out children. But because of the seriousness of the occasion, only one man walked with Kino, and that was his brother, Juan Tomás.

Juan Tomás cautioned his brother. "You must be careful to see they do not cheat you," he said.

And : "Very careful," Kino agreed.

"We do not know what prices are paid in other places," said Juan Tomás. "How can we know what is a fair price, if we do not know what the pearl buyer gets for the pearl in another place?"

"That is true," said Kino, "but how can we know? We are here, we are not there."

As they walked up towards the city the crowd grew behind them, and Juan Tomás, in pure nervousness, went on speaking.

"Before you were born, Kino," he said, "the old ones thought of a way to get more money for their pearls. They thought it would be better if they had an agent who took all the pearls to the capital and sold them there and kept only his share of the profit.

Kino nodded his head. "I know," he said. "It was a good thought."

"And so they got such a man," said Juan Tomás, "and they pooled the pearls, and they started him off. And he was never heard of again and the pearls were lost. Then they got another man, and they started him off, and he was never heard of again. And so they gave the whole thing up and went back to the old way."

"I know," said Kino. "I have heard our father tell of it. It was a good idea, but it was against religion, and the Father made that very clear. The loss of the pearl was a punishment visited on those who tried to leave their station. And the Father made it clear that each man and woman is like a soldier sent by God to guard some part of the castle of the Universe. And some are in the ramparts and some far deep in the darkness of the walls. But each one must remain faithful to his post and must not go

41

running about, else the castle is in danger from the assaults of Hell."

"I have heard him make that sermon," said Juan Tomás. "He makes it every year."

The brothers, as they walked along, squinted their eyes a little, as they and their grandfathers and their great-grandfathers had done for four hundred years, since first the strangers came with argument and authority and gun-powder to back up both. And in the four hundred years Kino's people had learned only one defence—a slight slitting of the eyes and a slight tightening of the lips and a retirement. Nothing could break down this wall, and they could remain whole within the wall.

The gathering procession was solemn, for they sensed the importance of this day, and any children who showed a tendency to scuffle, to scream, to cry out, to steal hats and rumple hair were hissed to silence by their elders. So important was this day that an old man came to see, riding on the stalwart shoulders of his nephew. The pro-cession left the brush huts and entered the stone-and-plaster city, where the streets were a little wider and there were narrow pavements beside the buildings. And as be-fore, the beggars joined them as they passed the church; the grocers looked out at them as they went by; the little saloons lost their customers, and the owners closed up shop and went along. And the sun beat down on the streets of the city and even tiny stones threw shadows on the ground.

The news of the approach of the procession ran ahead of it, and in their little dark offices the pearl buyers stiff-ened and grew alert. They got out papers so that they could be at work when Kino appeared, and they put their pearls in the desks, for it is not good to let an inferior pearl be seen beside a beauty. And word of the loveliness of Kino's pearl had come to them. The pearl buyers' offices were clustered together in one narrow street, and they were barred at the windows, and wooden slats cut out the light so that only a soft gloom entered the offices.

A stout slow man sat in an office waiting. His face was fatherly and benign, and his eyes twinkled with friendship. He was a caller of good mornings, a ceremonious shaker of hands, a jolly man who knew all jokes and yet who hovered close to sadness, for in the midst of a laugh he could remember the death of your aunt, and his eyes could become wet with sorrow for your loss. This morning he had placed a flower in a vase on his desk, a single scarlet hibiscus, and the vase sat beside the black velvet-lined pearl tray in front of him. He was shaved close to the blue roots of his beard, and his hands were clean and his nails polished. His door stood open to the morning, and he hummed under his breath while his right hand practised legerdemain. He rolled a coin back and forth over his knuckles and made it appear and disappear, made it spin and sparkle. The coin winked into sight and as quickly slipped out of sight, and the man did not even watch his own performance. The fingers did it all mechanically, precisely, while the man hummed to himself and peered out the door. Then he heard the tramp of feet of the approaching crowd, and the fingers of his right hand worked faster and faster until, as the figure of Kino filled the doorway, the coin flashed and disappeared.

"Good morning, my friend," the stout man said. "What can I do for you?"

Kino stared into the dimness of the little office, for his eyes were squeezed from the outside glare. But the buyer's eyes had become as steady and cruel and unwinking as a hawk's eyes, while the rest of his face smiled in greeting. And secretly, behind his desk, his right hand practised with the coin.

"I have a pearl," said Kino. And Juan Tomás stood beside him and snorted a little at the understatement. The neighbours peered around the doorway, and a line of little boys clambered on the window bars and looked through. Several little boys, on their hands and knees, watched the scene around Kino's legs.

"You have a pearl," the dealer said. "Sometimes a man

43

brings in a dozen. Well, let us see your pearl. We will value it and give you the best price." And his fingers worked furiously with the coin.

Now Kino instinctively knew his own dramatic effects. Slowly he brought out the leather bag, slowly took from it the soft and dirty piece of deerskin, and then he let the great pearl roll into the black velvet tray, and instantly his eyes went to the buyer's face. But there was no sign, no movement, the face did not change, but the secret hand behind the desk missed in its precision. The coin stumbled over a knuckle and slipped silently into the dealer's lap. And the fingers behind the desk curled into a fist. When the right hand came out of hiding, the forefinger touched the great pearl, rolled it on the black velvet; thumb and forefinger picked it up and brought it near to the dealer's eyes and twirled it in the air.

Kino held his breath, and the neighbours held their breath, and the whispering went back through the crowd. "He is inspecting it—No price has been mentioned yet— They have not come to a price."

Now the dealer's hand had become a personality. The hand tossed the great pearl back in the tray, the forefinger poked and insulted it, and on the dealer's face there came a sad and contemptuous smile.

"I am sorry, my friend," he said, and his shoulders rose a little to indicate that the misfortune was no fault of his.

"It is a pearl of great value," Kino said.

The dealer's fingers spurned the pearl so that it bounced and rebounded softly from the side of the velvet tray.

"You have heard of fool's gold," the dealer said. "This pearl is like fool's gold. It is too large. Who would buy it? There is no market for such things. It is a curiosity only. I am sorry. You thought it was a thing of value, and it is only a curiosity."

Now Kino's face was perplexed and worried. "It is the Pearl of the World," he cried. "No one has ever seen such a pearl."

"On the contrary," said the dealer, "it is large and

44

clumsy. As a curiosity it has interest; some museum might perhaps take it to place in a collection of sea-shells. I can give you, say, a thousand pesos."

Kino's face grew dark and dangerous. "It is worth fifty thousand," he said. "You know it. You want to cheat me."

And the dealer heard a little grumble go through the crowd as they heard his price. And the dealer felt a little tremor of fear.

"Do not blame me," he said quickly. "I am only an appraiser. Ask the others. Go to their offices and show your pearl—or better, let them come here, so that you can see there is no collusion. Boy," he called. And when his servant looked through the rear door : "Boy, go to such a one, and such another one and such a third one. Ask them to step in here and do not tell them why. Just say that I will be pleased to see them." And his right hand went behind the desk and pulled another coin from his pocket, and the coin rolled back and forth over the knuckles.

Kino's neighbours whispered together. They had been afraid of something like this. The pearl was large, but it had a strange colour. They had been suspicious of it from the first. And after all, a thousand pesos was not to be thrown away. It was comparative wealth to a man who was not wealthy. And suppose Kino took a thousand pesos. Only yesterday he had nothing.

But Kino had grown tight and hard. He felt the creeping of fate, the circling of wolves, the hover of vultures. He felt the evil coagulating about him, and he was helpless to protect himself. He heard in his ears the evil music. And on the black velvet the great pearl glistened, so that the dealer could not keep his eyes from it.

The crowd in the doorway wavered and broke and let the three pearl dealers through. The crowd was silent now, fearing to miss a word, to fail to see a gesture or an expression. Kino was silent and watchful. He felt a little tugging at his back, and he turned and looked in Juana's eyes, and when he looked away he had renewed strength.

The dealers did not glance at one another nor at the pearl. The man behind the desk said : "I have put a value on this pearl. The owner here does not think it fair. I will ask you to examine this—this thing and make an offer. Notice," he said to Kino, "I have not mentioned what I have offered."

The first dealer, dry and stringy, seemed now to see the pearl for the first time. He took it up, rolled it quickly between thumb and forefinger, and then cast it contemptuously back into the tray.

"Do not include me in the discussion," he said dryly. "I will make no offer at all. I do not want it. This is not a pearl—it is a monstrosity." His thin lips curled.

Now the second dealer, a little man with a shy soft voice, took up the pearl, and he examined it carefully. He took a glass from his pocket and inspected it under magnification. Then he laughed softly.

"Better pearls are made of paste," he said. "I know these things. This is soft and chalky, it will lose its colour and die in a few months. Look——" He offered the glass to Kino, showed him how to use it, and Kino, who had never seen a pearl's surface magnified, was shocked at the strange-looking surface.

The third dealer took the pearl from Kino's hands. "One of my clients likes such things," he said. "I will offer five hundred pesos, and perhaps I can sell it to my client for six hundred."

Kino reached quickly and snatched the pearl from his hand. He wrapped it in the deerskin and thrust it inside his shirt.

The man behind the desk said : "I'm a fool, I know, but my first offer stands. I still offer one thousand. What are you doing?" he asked, as Kino thrust the pearl out of sight.

"I am cheated," Kino cried fiercely. "My pearl is not for sale here. I will go, perhaps even to the capital."

Now the dealers glanced quickly at one another. They

knew they had played too hard; they knew they would be disciplined for their failure, and the man at the desk said quickly: "I might go to fifteen hundred."

But Kino was pushing his way through the crowd. The hum of talk came to him dimly, his rage blood pounded in his ears, and he burst through and strode away. Juana followed, trotting after him.

When the evening came, the neighbours in the brush houses sat eating their corn-cakes and beans, and they discussed the great theme of the morning. They did not know, it seemed a fine pearl to them, but they had never seen such a pearl before, and surely the dealers knew more about the value of pearls than they. "And mark this," they said. "Those dealers did not discuss these things. Each of the three knew the pearl was valueless."

"But suppose they had arranged it before?"

"If that is so, then all of us have been cheated all of our lives."

Perhaps, some argued, perhaps it would have been better if Kino took the one thousand five hundred pesos. That is a great deal of money, more than he has ever seen. Maybe Kino is being a pig-headed fool. Suppose he should really go to the capital and find no buyer for his pearl. He would never live that down.

And now, said other fearful ones, now that he has defied them, those buyers will not want to deal with him at all. Maybe Kino has cut off his own head and destroyed himself.

And others said, Kino is a brave man, and a fierce man; he is right. From his courage we may all profit. These were proud of Kino.

In his house Kino squatted on his sleeping-mat, brooding. He had buried his pearl under a stone of the fire hole in his house, and he stared at the woven tules of his sleeping-mat until the crossed design danced in his head. He had lost one world and had not gained another. And Kino was afraid. Never in his life had he been far from home. He was afraid of strangers and of strange places. He was terrified of the monster of strangeness they called the capital. It lay over the water and through the mountains, over a thousand miles, and every strange terrible mile was frightening. But Kino had lost his old world and he must clamber on to a new one. For his dream of the future was real and never to be destroyed, and he had said "I will go", and that made a real thing too. To determine to go and to say it was to be halfway there.

Juana watched him while he buried his pearl, and she watched him while she cleaned Coyotito and nursed him, and Juana made the corn-cakes for supper.

Juan Tomás came in and squatted down beside Kino and remained silent for a long time, until at last Kino demanded: "What else could I do? They are cheats."

Juan Tomás nodded gravely. He was the elder, and Kino looked to him for wisdom. "It is hard to know," he said. "We do know that we are cheated from birth to the overcharge on our coffins. But we survive. You have defied not the pearl buyers, but the whole structure, the whole way of life, and I am afraid for you."

"What have I to fear but starvation?" Kino asked.

But Juan Tomás shook his head slowly. "That we must all fear. But suppose you are correct—suppose your pearl is of great value—do you think then the game is over?"

"What do you mean?"

"I don't know," said Juan Tomás, "but I am afraid for you. It is a new ground you are walking on, you do not know the way."

"I will go. I will go soon," said Kino.

"Yes," Juan Tomás agreed. "That you must do. But I wonder if you will find it any different in the capital? Here, you have friends and me, your brother. There, you will have no one."

"What can I do?" Kino cried. "Some deep outrage is here. My son must have a chance. That is what they are striking at. My friends will protect me."

"Only so long as they are not in danger or discomfort

from it," said Juan Tomás. He arose, saying: "Go with God."

And Kino said: "Go with God," and did not even look up, for the words had a strange chill in them.

Long after Juan Tomás had gone Kino sat brooding on his sleeping-mat. A lethargy had settled on him, and a little grey hopelessness. Every road seemed blocked against him. In his head he heard only the dark music of the enemy. His senses were burningly alive, but his mind went back to the deep participation with all things, the gift he had from his people. He heard every little sound of the gathering night, the sleepy complaint of settling birds, the love agony of cats, the strike and withdrawal of little waves on the beach, and the simple hiss of distance. And he could smell the sharp odour of exposed kelp from the receding tide. The little flare of the twig fire made the design on his sleeping-mat jump before his entranced eyes.

Juana watched him with worry, but she knew him and she knew she could help him best by being silent and by being near. And as though she too could hear the Song of Evil, she fought it, singing softly the melody of the family, of the safety and warmth and wholeness of the family. She held Coyotito in her arms and sang the song to him, to keep the evil out, and her voice was brave against the threat of the dark music.

Kino did not move nor ask for his supper. She knew he would ask when he wanted it. His eyes were entranced, and he could sense the wary, watchful evil outside the brush house; he could feel the dark creeping things waiting for him to go out into the night. It was shadowy and dreadful, and yet it called to him and threatened him and challenged him. His right hand went into his shirt and felt his knife; his eyes were wide; he stood up and walked to the doorway.

Juana willed to stop him; she raised her hand to stop him, and her mouth opened with terror. For a long moment Kino looked out into the darkness and then he stepped outside. Juana heard the little rush, the grunting struggle, the blow. She froze with terror for a moment, and then her lips drew back from her teeth like a cat's lips. She set Coyotito down on the ground. She seized a stone from the fireplace and rushed outside, but it was over by then. Kino lay on the ground, struggling to rise, and there was no one near him. Only the shadows and the strike and rush of waves and the hiss of distance. But the evil was all about, hidden behind the brush fence, crouched beside the house in the shadow, hovering in the air.

Juana dropped her stone, and she put her arms around Kino and helped him to his feet and supported him into the house. Blood oozed down from his scalp and there was a long deep cut in his cheek from ear to chin, a deep, bleeding slash. And Kino was only half conscious. He shook his head from side to side. His shirt was torn open and his clothes half pulled off. Juana sat him down on his sleeping-mat and she wiped the thickening blood from his face with her skirt. She brought him pulque to drink in a little pitcher, and still he shook his head to clear out the darkness.

"Who?" Juana asked.

"I don't know," Kino said. "I didn't see."

Now Juana brought her clay pot of water and she washed the cut on his face while he stared dazed ahead of him.

"Kino, my husband," she cried, and his eyes stared past her. "Kino, can you hear me?"

"I hear you," he said dully.

"Kino, this pearl is evil. Let us destroy it before it destroys us. Let us crush it between two stones. Let us— let us throw it back in the sea where it belongs. Kino, it is evil, it is evil!"

And as she spoke the light came back in Kino's eyes so that they glowed fiercely and his muscles hardened and his will hardened.

"No," he said. "I will fight this thing. I will win over it. We will have our chance." His fist pounded the sleeping-mat. "No one shall take our good fortune from us," he said. His eyes softened then and he raised a gentle hand to Juana's shoulder. "Believe me," he said. "I am a man." And his face grew crafty.

"In the morning we will take our canoe and we will go over the sea and over the mountains to the capital, you and I. We will not be cheated. I am a man."

"Kino," she said huskily, "I am afraid. A man can be killed. Let us throw the pearl back into the sea."

"Hush," he said fiercely. "I am a man. Hush." And she was silent, for his voice was command. "Let us sleep a little," he said. "In the first light we will start. You are not afraid to go with me?"

"No, my husband."

His eyes were soft and warm on her then, his hand touched her cheek. "Let us sleep a little," he said.

V

THE late moon arose before the first rooster crowed. Kino opened his eyes in the darkness, for he sensed movement near him, but he did not move. Only his eyes searched the darkness, and in the pale light of the moon that crept through the holes in the brush house Kino saw Juana arise silently from beside him. He saw her move towards the fireplace. So carefully did she move that he heard only the lightest sound when she moved the fireplace stone. And then like a shadow she glided towards the door. She paused for a moment beside the hanging box where Coyotito lay, then for a second she was black in the doorway, and then she was gone.

And rage surged in Kino. He rolled up to his feet and followed her as silently as she had gone, and he could hear her quick footsteps going towards the shore. Quietly he tracked her, and his brain was red with anger. She burst clear of the brush line and stumbled over the little boulders towards the water, and then she heard him coming and she broke into a run. Her arm was up to throw when he leaped at her and caught her arm and wrenched the pearl from her. He struck her in the face with his clenched fist and she fell among the boulders, and he kicked her in the side. In the pale light he could see the little waves break over her, and her skirt floated about and clung to her legs as the water receded.

Kino looked down at her and his teeth were bared. He hissed at her like a snake, and Juana stared at him with wide unfrightened eyes, like a sheep before the butcher. She knew there was murder in him, and it was all right; she had accepted it, and she would not resist or even protest. And then the rage left him and a sick disgust took its place. He turned away from her and walked up the beach and through the brush line. His senses were dulled by his emotion.

He heard the rush, got his knife out and lunged at one dark figure and felt his knife go home, and then he was swept to his knees and swept again to the ground. Greedy fingers went through his clothes, frantic fingers searched him, and the pearl, knocked from his hand, lay winking behind a little stone in the pathway. It glinted in the soft moonlight.

Juana dragged herself up from the rocks on the edge of the water. Her face was a dull pain and her side ached. She steadied herself on her knees for a while and her wet skirt clung to her. There was no anger in her for Kino. He had said : "I am a man", and that meant certain things to Juana. It meant that he was half insane and half god. It meant that Kino would drive his strength against a mountain and plunge his strength against the sea. Juana, in her woman's soul, knew that the mountain would stand while the man broke himself; that the sea would surge while the man drowned in it. And yet it was this thing that made him a man, half insane and half god, and Juana had need of a man; she could not live without a man. Although she might be puzzled by these differences between man and woman, she knew them and accepted them and needed them. Of course she would follow him, there was no question of that. Sometimes the quality of woman, the reason, the caution, the sense of preservation, could cut through Kino's manness and save them all. She climbed painfully to her feet, and she dipped her cupped palms in the little waves and washed her bruised face with the stinging salt water, and then she went creeping up the beach after Kino.

A flight of herring clouds had moved over the sky from the south. The pale moon dipped in and out of the strands of clouds so that Juana walked in darkness for a moment and in light the next. Her back was bent with pain and her head was low. She went through the line of brush when the moon was covered, and when it looked through she saw the glimmer of the great pearl in the path behind the rock. She sank to her knees and picked it up, and the moon went into the darkness of the clouds again. Juana remained on her knees while she considered whether to go back to the sea and finish her job, and as she considered, the light came again, and she saw two dark figures lying in the path ahead of her. She leaped forward and saw that one was Kino and the other a stranger with dark shiny fluid leaking from his throat.

Kino moved sluggishly, arms and legs stirred like those of a crushed bug, and a thick muttering came from his mouth. Now, in an instant, Juana knew that the old life was gone forever. A dead man in the path and Kino's knife, dark-bladed beside him, convinced her. All the time Juana had been trying to rescue something of the old peace, of the time before the pearl. But now it was gone, and there was no retrieving it. And knowing this, she abandoned the past instantly. There was nothing to do but to save themselves.

Her pain was gone now, her slowness. Quickly she dragged the dead man from the pathway into the shelter of the brush. She went to Kino and sponged his face with her wet skirt. His senses were coming back and he moaned.

"They have taken the pearl. I have lost it. Now it is over," he said. "The pearl is gone."

Juana quieted him as she would quiet a sick child. "Hush," she said. "Here is your pearl. I found it in the path. Can you hear me now? Here is your pearl. Can you understand? You have killed a man. We must go away. They will come for us, can you understand? We must be gone before the daylight comes."

"I was attacked," Kino said uneasily. "I struck to save my life."

"Do you remember yesterday?" Juana asked. "Do you think that will matter? Do you remember the men of the city? Do you think your explanation will help?"

Kino drew a great breath and fought off his weakness. "No," he said. "You are right." And his will hardened and he was a man again.

"Go to our house and bring Coyotito," he said, "and bring all the corn we have. I will drag the canoe into the water and we will go."

He took his knife and left her. He stumbled towards the beach and he came to his canoe. And when the light broke through again he saw that a great hole had been knocked in the bottom. And a searing rage came to him and gave him strength. Now the darkness was closing in on his family; now the evil music filled the night, hung over the mangroves, skirled in the wave beat. The canoe of his grandfather, plastered over and over, and a splintered hole broken in it. This was an evil beyond thinking. The killing of a man was not so evil as the killing of a boat. For a boat does not have sons, and a boat cannot protect itself, and a wounded boat does not heal. There was sorrow in Kino's rage, but this last thing had tightened him beyond breaking. He was an animal now, for hiding, for attacking, and he lived only to preserve himself and his family. He was not conscious of the pain in his head. He leaped up the beach, through the brush line towards his brush house, and it did not occur to him to take one of the canoes of his neighbours. Never once did the thought enter his head, any more than he could have conceived breaking a boat.

The roosters were crowing and the dawn was not far off. Smoke of the first fires seeped out through the walls of the brush houses, and the first smell of cooking corn-cakes was in the air. Already the dawn birds were scampering in the bushes. The weak moon was losing its light and the clouds thickened and curdled to the southward. The wind blew freshly into the estuary, a nervous, restless wind with the smell of storm on its breath, and there was change and uneasiness in the air.

Kino, hurrying towards his house, felt a surge of exhilaration. Now he was not confused, for there was only one thing to do, and Kino's hand went first to the great pearl in his shirt and then to his knife hanging under his shirt.

He saw a little glow ahead of him, and then without interval a tall flame leaped up in the dark with a crackling roar, and a tall edifice of fire lighted the pathway. Kino broke into a run; it was his brush house, he knew. And he knew that these houses could burn down in a very few moments. And as he ran a scuttling figure ran towards him—Juana, with Coyotito in her arms and Kino's shoulder-blanket clutched in her hand. The baby moaned with fright, and Juana's eyes were wide and terrified. Kino could see the house was gone, and he did not question Juana. He knew, but she said : "It was torn up and the floor dug—even the baby's box turned out, and as I looked they put the fire to the outside."

The fierce light of the burning house lighted Kino's face strongly. "Who?" he demanded.

"I don't know," she said. "The dark ones."

The neighbours were tumbling from their houses now, and they watched the falling sparks and stamped them out to save their own houses. Suddenly Kino was afraid. The light made him afraid. He remembered the man lying dead in the brush beside the path, and he took Juana by the arm and drew her into the shadow of a house away

55

from the light, for light was danger to him. For a moment he considered and then he worked among the shadows until he came to the house of Juan Tomás, his brother, and he slipped into the doorway and drew Juana after him. Outside he could hear the squeal of children and the shouts of the neighbours, for his friends thought he might be inside the burning house.

The house of Juan Tomás was almost exactly like Kino's house; nearly all the brush houses were alike, and all leaked light and air, so that Juana and Kino, sitting in the corner of the brother's house, could see the leaping flames through the wall. They saw the flames tall and furious, they saw the roof fall and watched the fire die down as quickly as a twig fire dies. They heard the cries of warning of their friends, and the shrill, keening cry of Apolonia, wife of Juan Tomás. She, being the nearest woman relative, raised a formal lament for the dead of the family.

Apolonia realized that she was wearing her second-best head-shawl and she rushed to her house to get her fine new one. As she rummaged in a box by the wall, Kino's voice said quietly : "Apolonia, do not cry out. We are not hurt."

"How do you come here?" she demanded.

"Do not question," he said. "Go now to Juan Tomás and bring him here and tell no one else. This is important to us, Apolonia."

She paused, her hands helpless in front of her, and then : "Yes, my brother-in-law," she said.

In a few moments Juan Tomás came back with her. He lighted a candle and came to them where they crouched in a corner, and he said : "Apolonia, see to the door, and do not let anyone enter." He was older, Juan Tomás, and he assumed the authority. "Now, my brother," he said.

"I was attacked in the dark," said Kino. "And in the fight I have killed a man."

"Who?" asked Juan Tomás quickly.

"I do not know. It is all darkness—all darkness and shape of darkness."

56

"It is the pearl," said Juan Tomás. "There is a devil in this pearl. You should have sold it and passed on the devil. Perhaps you can still sell it and buy peace for yourself."

And Kino said : "Oh, my brother, an insult has been put on me that is deeper than my life. For on the beach my canoe is broken, my house is burned, and in the brush a dead man lies. Every escape is cut off. You must hide us, my brother."

And Kino, looking closely, saw deep worry come into his brother's eyes and he forestalled him in a possible refusal. "Not for long," he said quickly. "Only until a day has passed and the new light has come. Then we will go."

"I will hide you," said Juan Tomás.

"I do not want to bring danger to you," Kino said. "I know I am like a leprosy. I will go tonight and then you will be safe."

"I will protect you," said Juan Tomás, and he called : "Apolonia, close up the door. Do not even whisper that Kino is here."

They sat silently all day in the darkness of the house, and they could hear the neighbours speaking of them. Through the walls of the house they could watch their neighbours raking through the ashes to find the bones. Crouching in the house of Juan Tomás, they heard the shock go into their neighbours' minds at the news of the broken boat. Juan Tomás went out among the neighbours to divert their suspicions, and he gave them theories and ideas of what had happened to Kino and to Juana and to the baby. To one he said : "I think they have gone south along the coast to escape the evil that was on them." And to another : "Kino would never leave the sea. Perhaps he found another boat." And he said : "Apolonia is ill with grief."

And in that day the wind rose up to beat the Gulf and tore the kelps and weeds that lined the shore, and the wind cried through the brush houses and no boat was safe on the water. Then Juan Tomás told among the neighbours : "Kino is gone. If he went to the sea, he is drowned by now." And after each trip among the neighbours Juan Tomás came back with something borrowed. He brought a little woven straw bag of red beans and a gourd full of rice. He borrowed a cup of dried peppers and a block of salt, and he brought in a long working knife, eighteen inches long and heavy, as a small axe, a tool and a weapon. And when Kino saw this knife his eyes lighted up, and he fondled the blade and his thumb tested the edge.

The wind screamed over the Gulf and turned the water white, and the mangroves plunged like frightened cattle, and a fine sandy dust arose from the land and hung in a stifling cloud over the sea. The wind drove off the clouds and skimmed the sky clean and drifted the sand of the country like snow.

Then Juan Tomás, when the evening approached, talked long with his brother. "Where will you go?"

"To the north," said Kino. "I have heard that there are cities in the north."

"Avoid the shore," said Juan Tomás. "They are making a party to search the shore. The men in the city will look for you. Do you still have the pearl?"

"I have it," said Kino. "And I will keep it. I might have given it as a gift, but now it is my misfortune and my life and I will keep it." His eyes were hard and cruel and bitter.

Coyotito whimpered and Juana muttered little magics over him to make him silent.

"The wind is good," said Juan Tomás. "There will be no tracks."

They left quietly in the dark before the moon had risen. The family stood formally in the house of Juan Tomás. Juana carried Coyotito on her back, covered and held in by her head-shawl, and the baby slept, cheek turned sideways against her shoulder. The head-shawl covered the baby, and one end of it came across Juana's nose to protect her from the evil night air. Juan Tomás embraced his brother with the double embrace and kissed him on both cheeks. "Go with God," he said, and it was like a death. "You will not give up the pearl?"

"This pearl has become my soul," said Kino. "If I give it up I shall lose my soul. Go thou also with God."

VI

THE wind blew fierce and strong, and it pelted them with bits of sticks, sand, and little rocks. Juana and Kino gathered their clothing tighter about them and covered their noses and went out into the world. The sky was brushed clean by the wind and the stars were cold in a black sky. The two walked carefully, and they avoided the centre of the town, where some sleeper in a doorway might see them pass. For the town closed itself in against the night, and anyone who moved about in the darkness would be noticeable. Kino threaded his way around the edge of the city and turned north, north by the stars, and found the rutted sandy road that led through the brushy country road towards Loreto, where the miraculous Virgin has her station.

Kino could feel the blown sand against his ankles and he was glad, for he knew there would be no tracks. The little light from the stars made out for him the narrow road through the brushy country. And Kino could hear the pad of Juana's feet behind him. He went quickly and quietly, and Juana trotted behind him to keep up.

Some ancient thing stirred in Kino. Through his fear of dark and the devils that haunt the night, there came a rush of exhilaration; some animal thing was moving in him so that he was cautious and wary and dangerous; some ancient thing out of the past of his people was alive in him. The wind was at his back and the stars guided him. The wind cried and whisked in the brush and the family went on monotonously, hour after hour. They passed no one and saw no one. At last, to their right, the

59

waning moon arose, and when it came up the wind died down, and the land was still.

Now they could see the little road ahead of them, deep cut with sand-drifted wheel-tracks. With the wind gone there would be footprints, but they were a good distance from the town and perhaps their tracks might not be noticed. Kino walked carefully in a wheel-rut, and Juana followed in his path. One big cart, going to the town in the morning, could wipe out every trace of their passage.

All night they walked and never changed their pace. Once Coyotito awakened, and Juana shifted him in front of her and soothed him until he went to sleep again. And the evils of the night were about them. The coyotes cried and laughed in the brush, and the owls screeched and hissed over their heads. And once some large animal lumbered away, crackling the undergrowth as it went. And Kino gripped the handle of the big working knife and took a sense of protection from it.

The music of the pearl was triumphant in Kino's head, and the quiet melody of the family underlay it, and they wove themselves into the soft padding of sandalled feet in the dust. All night they walked, and in the first dawn Kino searched the roadside for a covert to lie in during the day. He found his place near to the road, a little clearing where deer might have lain, and it was curtained thickly with the dry brittle trees that lined the road. And when Juana had seated herself and had settled to nurse the baby, Kino went back to the road. He broke a branch and carefully swept the footprints where they had turned from the roadway. And then, in the first light, he heard the creak of a wagon, and he crouched beside the road and watched a heavy two-wheeled cart go by, drawn by slouching oxen. And when it had passed out of sight, he went back to the roadway and looked at the rut and found that the footprints were gone. And again he swept out his traces and went back to Juana.

She gave him the soft corn-cakes Apolonia had packed for them, and after a while she slept a little. But Kino sat on the ground and stared at the earth in front of him. He watched the ants moving, a little column of them near to his foot, and he put his foot in their path. Then the column climbed over his instep and continued on its way, and Kino left his foot there and watched them move over it.

The sun arose hotly. They were not near the Gulf now, and the air was dry and hot so that the brush cricked with heat and a good resinous smell came from it. And when Juana awakened, when the sun was high, Kino told her things she knew already.

"Beware of that kind of tree there," he said, pointing. "Do not touch it, for if you do and then touch your eyes, it will blind you. And beware of the tree that bleeds. See, that one over there. For if you break it the red blood will flow from it, and it is evil luck." And she nodded and smiled a little at him, for she knew these things.

"Will they follow us?" she asked. "Do you think they will try to find us?"

"They will try," said Kino. "Whoever finds us will take the pearl. Oh, they will try."

And Juana said : "Perhaps the dealers were right and the pearl has no value. Perhaps this has all been an illusion."

Kina reached into his clothes and brought out the pearl. He let the sun play on it until it burned in his eyes. "No," he said, "they would not have tried to steal it if it had been valueless."

"Do you know who attacked you? Was it the dealers?"

"I do not know," he said. "I didn't see them."

He looked into his pearl to find his vision. "When we sell it at last, I will have a rifle," he said, and he looked into the shining surface for his rifle, but he saw only a huddled dark body on the ground with shining blood dripping from its throat. And he said quickly : "We will be married in a great church." And in the pearl he saw Juana with her beaten face crawling home through the night. "Our son must learn to read," he said frantically.

And there in the pearl Coyotito's face, thick and feverish from the medicine.

And Kino thrust the pearl back into his clothing, and the music of the pearl had become sinister in his ears, and it was interwoven with the music of evil.

The hot sun beat on the earth so that Kino and Juana moved into the lacy shade of the brush, and small grey birds scampered on the ground in the shade. In the heat of the day Kino relaxed and covered his eyes with his hat and wrapped his blanket about his face to keep the flies off, and he slept.

But Juana did not sleep. She sat quiet as a stone and her face was quiet. Her mouth was still swollen where Kino had struck her, and big flies buzzed around the cut on her chin. But she sat as still as a sentinel, and when Coyotito awakened she placed him on the ground in front of her and watched him wave his arms and kick his feet, and he smiled and gurgled at her until she smiled too. She picked up a little twig from the ground and tickled him, and she gave him water from the gourd she carried in her bundle.

Kino stirred in a dream, and he cried out in a guttural voice, and his hand moved in symbolic fighting. And then he moaned and sat up suddenly, his eyes wide and his nostrils flaring. He listened and heard only the cricking heat and the hiss of distance.

"What is it?" Juana asked.

"Hush," he said.

"You were dreaming."

"Perhaps." But he was restless, and when she gave him a corn-cake from her store he paused in his chewing to listen. He was uneasy and nervous; he glanced over his shoulder; he lifted the big knife and felt its edge. When Coyotito gurgled on the ground Kino said: "Keep him quiet."

"What is the matter?" Juana asked.

"I don't know."

He listened again, an animal light in his eyes. He stood

up then, silently; and crouched low, he threaded his way through the brush towards the road. But he did not step into the road; he crept into the cover of a thorny tree and peered out along the way he had come.

And then he saw them moving along. His body stiffened and he drew down his head and peeked out from under a fallen branch. In the distance he could see three figures, two on foot and one on horseback. But he knew what they were, and a chill of fear went through him. Even in the distance he could see the two on foot moving slowly along, bent low to the ground. Here, one would pause and look at the earth, while the other joined him. They were the trackers, they could follow the trail of a bighorn sheep in the stone mountains. They were as sensitive as hounds. Here, he and Juana might have stepped out of the wheel rut, and these people from the inland, these hunters, could read a broken straw or a little tumbled pile of dust. Behind them, on a horse, was a dark man, his nose covered with a blanket, and across his saddle a rifle gleamed in the sun.

Kino lay as rigid as the tree limb. He barely breathed, and his eyes went to the place where he had swept out the track. Even the sweeping might be a message to the trackers. He knew these inland hunters. In a country where there was little game they managed to live because of their ability to hunt, and they were hunting him. They scuttled over the ground like animals and found a sign and crouched over it while the horseman waited.

The trackers whined a little, like excited dogs on a warming trail. Kino slowly drew his big knife to his hand and made it ready. He knew what he must do. If the trackers found the swept place, he must leap for the horseman, kill him quickly and take the rifle. That was his only chance in the world. And as the three drew nearer on the road, Kino dug little pits with his sandalled toes so that he could leap without warning, so that his feet would not slip. He had only a little vision under the fallen limb.

Now Juana, back in her hidden place, heard the pad of

the horse's hoofs, and Coyotito gurgled. She took him up quickly and put him under her shawl and gave him her breast and he was silent.

When the trackers came near, Kino could see only their legs and only the legs of the horse from under the fallen branch. He saw the dark horny feet of the men and their ragged white clothes, and he heard the creak of leather of the saddle and the clink of spurs. The trackers stopped at the swept place and studied it, and the horseman stopped. The horse flung his head up against the bit and the bit-roller clicked under his tongue and the horse snorted. Then the dark trackers turned and studied the horse and watched his ears.

Kino was not breathing, but his back arched a little and the muscles of his arms and legs stood out with tension and a line of sweat formed on his upper lip. For a long moment the trackers bent over the road, and then they moved on slowly, studying the ground ahead of them, and the horseman moved after them. The trackers scuttled along, stopping, looking, and hurrying on. They would be back, Kino knew. They would be circling and searching, peeping, stooping, and they would come back sooner or later to his covered track.

He slid backwards and did not bother to cover his tracks. He could not; too many little signs were there, too many broken twigs and scuffed places and displaced stones. And there was a panic in Kino now, a panic of flight. The trackers would find his trail, he knew it. There was no escape, except in flight. He edged away from the road and went quickly and silently to the hidden place where Juana was. She looked up at him in question.

"Trackers," he said. "Come!"

And then a helplessness and a hopelessness swept over him, and his face went blank and his eyes were sad. "Perhaps I should let them take me."

Instantly Juana was on her feet and her hand lay on his arm. "You have the pearl," she cried hoarsely. "Do you think they would take you back alive to say they had stolen it?"

His hand strayed limply to the place where the pearl was hidden under his clothes. "They will find it," he said weakly.

"Come," she said. "Come!"

And when he did not respond, "Do you think they would let me live? Do you think they would let the little one here live?"

Her goading struck into his brain; his lips snarled and his eyes were fierce again. "Come," he said. "We will go into the mountains. Maybe we can lose them in the mountains."

Frantically he gathered the gourds and the little bags that were their property. Kino carried a bundle in his left hand, but the big knife swung free in his right hand. He parted the brush for Juana and they hurried to the west, towards the high stone mountains. They trotted quickly through the tangle of the undergrowth. This was panic flight. Kino did not try to conceal his passage; he trotted, kicking the stones, knocking the tell-tale leaves from the little trees. The high sun streamed down on the dry creaking earth so that even the vegetation ticked in protest. But ahead were the naked granite mountains, rising out of erosion rubble and standing monolithic against the sky. And Kino ran for the high place, as nearly all animals do when they are pursued.

This land was waterless, furred with the cacti which could store water and with the great-rooted brush which could reach deep into the earth for a little moisture and get along on very little. And underfoot was not soil but broken rock, split into small cubes, great slabs, but none of it water-rounded. Little tufts of sad dry grass grew between the stones, grass that had sprouted with one single rain and headed, dropped its seed, and died. Horned toads watched the family go by and turned their little pivoting dragon heads. And now and then a great jack-rabbit, disturbed in his shape, bumped away and hid behind the nearest rock. The singing heat lay over this desert country, and ahead the stone mountains looked cool and welcoming.

And Kino fled. He knew what would happen. A little way along the road the trackers would become aware that they had missed the path, and they would come back, searching and judging, and in a little while they would find the place where Kino and Juana had rested. From there it would be easy for them—these little stones, the fallen leaves and the whipped branches, the scuffed places where a foot had slipped. Kino could see them in his mind, slipping along the track, whining a little with eagerness, and behind them, dark and half interested, the horseman with the rifle. His work would come last, for he would not take them back. Oh, the music of evil sang loud in Kino's head now, it sang with the whine of heat and with the dry ringing of snake rattles. It was not large and overwhelming now, but secret and poisonous, and the pounding of his heart gave it undertone and rhythm.

The way began to rise, and as it did the rocks grew larger. But now Kino had put a little distance between his family and the trackers. Now, on the first rise, he rested. He climbed a great boulder and looked back over the shimmering country, but he could not see his enemies, not even the tall horseman riding through the brush. Juana had squatted in the shade of the boulder. She raised her bottle of water to Coyotito's lips; his little dried tongue sucked greedily at it. She looked up at Kino when he came back; she saw him examine her ankles, cut and scratched from the stones and brush, and she covered them quickly with her skirt. Then she handed the bottle to him, but he shook his head. Her eyes were bright in her tired face. Kino moistened his cracked lips with his tongue.

"Juana," he said, "I will go on and you will hide. I will lead them into the mountains, and when they have gone past, you will go north to Loreto or to Santa Rosalia.

Then, if I can escape them, I will come to you. It is the only safe way."

She looked full into his eyes for a moment. "No," she said. "We go with you."

"I can go faster alone," he said harshly. "You will put the little one in more danger if you go with me."

"No," said Juana.

"You must. It is the wise thing and it is my wish," he said.

"No," said Juana.

He looked then for weakness in her face, for fear or irresolution, and there was none. Her eyes were very bright. He shrugged his shoulders helplessly then, but he had taken strength from her. When they moved on it was no longer panic flight.

The country, as it rose toward the mountains, changed rapidly. Now there were long outcroppings of granite with deep crevices between, and Kino walked on bare unmarkable stone when he could and leaped from ledge to ledge. He knew that wherever the trackers lost his path they must circle and lose time before they found it again. And so he did not go straight for the mountains any more; he moved in zigzags, and sometimes he cut back to the south and left a sign and then went towards the mountains over bare stone again. And the path rose steeply now, so that he panted a little as he went.

The sun moved downward toward the bare stone teeth of the mountains, and Kino set his direction for a dark and shadowy cleft in the range. If there were any water at all, it would be there, where he could see, even in the distance, a hint of foliage. And if there were any passage through the smooth stone range, it would be by this same deep cleft. It had its danger, for the trackers would think of it too, but the empty water-bottle did not let that consideration enter. And as the sun lowered, Kino and Juana struggled wearily up the steep slope towards the cleft.

High in the grey stone mountains, under a frowning peak, a little spring bubbled out of a rupture in the stone.

It was fed by shade-preserved snow in the summer, and now and then it died completely and bare rocks and dry algae were on its bottom. But nearly always it gushed out, cold and clean and lovely. In the times when the quick rains fell, it might become a freshet and send its column of white water crashing down the mountain cleft, but nearly always it was a lean little spring. It bubbled out into a pool and then fell a hundred feet to another pool, and this one, overflowing, dropped again, so that it continued, down and down, until it disappeared altogether. There wasn't much left of it then anyway, for every time it fell over an escarpment the thirsty air drank it, and it splashed from the pools to the dry vegetation. The animals from miles around came to drink from the little pools, and the wild sheep and the deer, the pumas and raccoons, and the mice—all came to drink. And the birds which spent the day in the brushland came at night to the little pools that were like steps in the mountain cleft. Beside this tiny stream, wherever enough earth collected for root-hold, colonies of plants grew, wild grape and little palms, maidenhair fern, hibiscus, and tall pampas grass with feathery rods raised above the spike leaves. And in the pool lived frogs and water-skaters, and water-worms crawled on the bottom of the pool. Everything that loved water came to these few shallow places. The cats took their prey there, and strewed feathers and lapped water through their bloody teeth. The little pools were places of life because of the water, and places of killing because of the water, too.

The lowest step, where the stream collected before it tumbled down a hundred feet and disappeared into the rubbly desert, was a little platform of stone and sand. Only a pencil of water fell into the pool, but it was enough to keep the pool full and to keep the ferns green in the underhang of the cliff, and wild grape climbed the stone mountain and all manner of little plants found comfort here. The freshets had made a small sandy beach through which the pool flowed, and bright-green watercress grew in the damp sand. The beach was cut and scarred and padded by the feet of animals that had come to drink and to hunt.

The sun had passed over the stone mountains when Kino and Juana struggled up the steep broken slope and came at last to the water. From this step they could look out over the sun-beaten desert to the blue Gulf in the distance. They came utterly weary to the pool, and Juana slumped to her knees and first washed Coyotito's face and then filled her bottle and gave him a drink. And the baby was weary and petulant, and he cried softly until Juana gave him her breast, and then he gurgled and clucked against her. Kino drank long and thirstily at the pool. For a moment, then, he stretched out beside the water and relaxed all his muscles and watched Juana feeding the baby, and then he got to his feet and went to the edge of the step where the water slipped over, and he searched the distance carefully. His eyes set on a point and he became rigid. Far down the slope he could see the two trackers; they were little more than dots or scurrying ants and behind them a larger ant.

Juana had turned to look at him and she saw his back stiffen.

"How far?" she asked quietly.

"They will be here by evening," said Kino. He looked up the long steep chimney of the cleft where the water came down. "We must go west," he said, and his eyes searched the stone shoulder behind the cleft. And thirty feet up on the grey shoulder he saw a series of little erosion caves. He slipped off his sandals and clambered up to them, gripping the bare stone with his toes, and he looked into the shallow caves. They were only a few feet deep, wind-hollowed scoops, but they sloped slightly downwards and back. Kino crawled into the largest one and lay down and knew that he could not be seen from the outside. Quickly he went back to Juana.

"You must go up there. Perhaps they will not find us there," he said.

Without question she filled her water-bottle to the top, and then Kino helped her up to the shallow cave and brought up the packages of food and passed them to her. And Juana sat in the cave entrance and watched him. She saw that he did not try to erase their tracks in the sand. Instead, he climbed up the brush cliff beside the water, clawing and tearing at the ferns and wild grape as he went. And when he had climbed a hundred feet to the next bench, he came down again. He looked carefully at the smooth rock shoulder towards the cave to see that there was no trace of passage, and last he climbed up and crept into the cave beside Juana.

"When they go up," he said, "we will slip away, down to the lowlands again. I am afraid only that the baby may cry. You must see that he does not cry."

"He will not cry," she said, and she raised the baby's face to her own and looked into his eyes and he stared solemnly back at her.

"He knows," said Juana.

Now Kino lay in the cave entrance, his chin braced on his crossed arms, and he watched the blue shadow of the mountain move out across the brushy desert below until it reached the Gulf, and the long twilight of the shadow was over the land.

The trackers were long in coming, as though they had trouble with the trail Kino had left. It was dusk when they came at last to the little pool. And all three were on foot now, for a horse could not climb the last steep slope. From above they were thin figures in the evening. The two trackers scurried about on the little beach, and they saw Kino's progress up the cliff before they drank. The man with the rifle sat down and rested himself, and the trackers squatted near him, and in the evening the points of their cigarettes glowed and receded. And then Kino could see that they were eating, and the soft murmur of their voices came to him.

Then darkness fell, deep and black in the mountain cleft. The animals that used the pool came near and smelled men there and drifted away again into the darkness.

He heard a murmur behind him. Juana was whispering: "Coyotito." She was begging him to be quiet. Kino heard the baby whimper, and he knew from the muffled sounds that Juana had covered his head with her shawl.

Down on the beach a match flared, and in its momentary light Kino saw that two of the men were sleeping, curled up like dogs, while the third watched, and he saw the glint of the rifle in the match light. And then the match died, but it left a picture on Kino's eyes. He could see it, just how each man was, two sleeping curled up and the third squatting in the sand with the rifle between his knees.

Kino moved silently back into the cave. Juana's eyes were two sparks reflecting a low star. Kino crawled quietly close to her and he put his lips near to her cheek.

"There is a way," he said.

"But they will kill you."

"If I get first to the one with the rifle," Kino said, "I must get to him first, then I will be all right. Two are sleeping."

Her hand crept out from under her shawl and gripped his arm. "They will see your white clothes in the starlight."

"No," he said. "And I must go before moonrise."

He searched for a soft word and then gave it up. "If they kill me," he said, "lie quietly. And when they are gone away, go to Loreto."

Her hand shook a little, holding his wrist.

"There is no choice," he said. "It is the only way. They will find us in the morning."

Her voice trembled a little. "Go with God," she said.

He peered closely at her and he could see her large eyes. His hand fumbled out and found the baby, and for a moment his palm lay on Coyotito's head. And then Kino raised his hand and touched Juana's cheek, and she held her breath.

Against the sky in the cave entrance Juana could see

that Kino was taking off his white clothes, for dirty and ragged though they were they would show up against the dark night. His own brown skin was a better protection for him. And then she saw how he hooked his amulet neck-string about the horn handle of his great knife, so that it hung down in front of him and left both hands free. He did not come back to her. For a moment his body was black in the cave entrance, crouched and silent, and then he was gone.

Juana moved to the entrance and looked out. She peered like an owl from the hole in the mountain, and the baby slept under the blanket on her back, his face turned sideways against her neck and shoulder. She could feel his warm breath against her skin, and Juana whispered her combination of prayer and magic, her Hail Marys and her ancient intercession, against the black inhuman things.

The night seemed a little less dark when she looked out, and to the east there was a lightening in the sky, down near the horizon where the moon would show. And, looking down, she could see the cigarette of the man on watch.

Kino edged like a slow lizard down the smooth rock shoulder. He had turned his neck-string so that the great knife hung down from his back and could not clash against the stone. His spread fingers gripped the mountain, and his bare toes found support through contact, and even his chest lay against the stone so that he would not slip. For any sound, a rolling pebble or a sigh, a little slip of flesh on rock, would rouse the watchers below. Any sound that was not germane to the night would make them alert. But the night was not silent; the little tree frogs that lived near the stream twittered like birds, and the high metallic ringing of the cicadas filled the mountain cleft. And Kino's own music was in his head, the music of the enemy, low and pulsing, nearly asleep. But the Song of the Family had become as fierce and sharp and feline as the snarl of a female puma. The family song was alive now and driving him down on the dark enemy. The harsh cicada seemed to take up its melody, and the twittering tree frogs called little phrases of it.

And Kino crept silently as a shadow down the smooth mountain face. One bare foot moved a few inches and the toes touched the stone and gripped, and the other foot a few inches, and then the palm of one hand a little downwards, and then the other hand, until the whole body, without seeming to move, had moved. Kino's mouth was open so that even his breath would make no sound, for he knew that he was not invisible. If the watcher, sensing movement, looked at the dark place against the stone which was his body, he could see him. Kino must move so slowly he would not draw the watcher's eyes. It took him a long time to reach the bottom and to crouch behind a little dwarf palm. His heart thundered in his chest and his hands and face were wet with sweat. He crouched and took great slow long breaths to calm himself.

Only twenty feet separated him from the enemy now, and he tried to remember the ground between. Was there any stone which might trip him in his rush? He kneaded his legs against cramp and found that his muscles were jerking after their long tension. And then he looked apprehensively to the east. The moon would rise in a few moments now, and he must attack before it rose. He could see the outline of the watcher, but the sleeping men were below his vision. It was the watcher Kino must find— must find quickly and without hesitation. Silently he drew the amulet string over his shoulder and loosened the loop from the horn handle of his great knife.

He was too late, for as he rose from his crouch the silver edge of the moon slipped above the eastern horizon, and Kino sank back behind his bush.

It was an old and ragged moon, but it threw hard light and hard shadow into the mountain cleft, and now Kino could see the seated figure of the watcher on the little beach beside the pool. The watcher gazed full at the moon, and then he lighted another cigarette, and the match illumined his dark face for a moment. There could be no waiting now; when the watcher turned his head, Kino must leap. His legs were as tight as wound springs.

And then from above came a little murmuring cry. The watcher turned his head to listen and then he stood up, and one of the sleepers stirred on the ground and awakened and asked quietly : "What is it?"

"I don't know," said the watcher. "It sounded like a cry, almost like a human—like a baby."

The man who had been sleeping said : "You can't tell. Some coyote bitch with a litter. I've heard a coyote pup cry like a baby."

The sweat rolled in drops down Kino's forehead and fell into his eyes and burned them. The little cry came again and the watcher looked up the side of the hill to the dark cave.

"Coyote maybe," he said, and Kino heard the harsh click as he cocked the rifle.

"If it's a coyote, this will stop it," the watcher said as he raised the gun.

Kino was in mid-leap when the gun crashed and the barrel-flash made a picture on his eyes. The great knife swung and crunched hollowly. It bit through neck and deep into chest, and Kino was a terrible machine now. He grasped the rifle as he wrenched free his knife. His strength and his movement and his speed were a machine. He whirled and struck the head of the seated man like a melon. The third man scrabbled away like a crab, slipped into the pool, and then he began to climb frantically, to climb up the cliff where the water pencilled down. His hands and feet threshed in the tangle of the wild grape-vine, and he whimpered and gibbered as he tried to get up. But Kino had become as cold and deadly as steel. Deliberately he threw the lever of the rifle, and then he raised the gun and aimed deliberately and fired. He saw his enemy tumble backwards into the pool, and Kino strode to the water. In the moonlight he could see the frantic frightened eyes, and Kino aimed and fired between the eyes.

74

And then Kino stood uncertainly. Something was wrong, some signal was trying to get through to his brain. Tree frogs and cicadas were silent now. And then Kino's brain cleared from its red concentration and he knew the sound—the keening, moaning, rising hysterical cry from the little cave in the side of the stone mountain, the cry of death.

Everyone in La Paz remembers the return of the family; there may be some old ones who saw it, but those whose fathers and whose grandfathers told it to them remember it nevertheless. It is an event that happened to everyone.

It was late in the golden afternoon when the first little boys ran hysterically into the town and spread the word that Kino and Juana were coming back. And everyone hurried to see them. The sun was settling towards the western mountains and the shadows on the ground were long. And perhaps that was what left the deep impression on those who saw them.

The two came from the rutted country road into the city, and they were not walking in single file, Kino ahead and Juana behind, as usual, but side by side. The sun was behind them and their long shadows stalked ahead, and they seemed to carry two towers of darkness with them. Kino had a rifle across his arm and Juana carried her shawl like a sack over her shoulder. And in it was a small limp heavy bundle. The shawl was crusted with dried blood, and the bundle swayed a little as she walked. Her face was hard and lined and leathery with fatigue and with the tightness with which she fought fatigue. And her wide eyes stared inwards on herself. She was as remote and as removed as Heaven. Kino's lips were thin and his jaws tight, and the people say that he carried fear with him, that he was as dangerous as a rising storm. The people say that the two seemed to be removed from human experience; that they had gone through pain and had come out on the other side; that there was almost a magical protection about them. And those people who had rushed to see them crowded back and let them pass and did not speak to them.

Kino and Juana walked through the city as though it were not there. Their eyes glanced neither right nor left nor up nor down, but stared only straight ahead. Their legs moved a little jerkily, like well-made wooden dolls, and they carried pillars of black fear about them. And as they walked through the stone-and-plaster city brokers peered at them from barred windows and servants put one eye to a slitted gate and mothers turned the faces of their youngest children inwards against their skirts. Kino and Juana strode side by side through the stone-and-plaster city and down among the brush houses, and the neighbours stood back and let them pass. Juan Tomás raised his hand in greeting and did not say the greeting and left his hand in the air for a moment uncertainly.

In Kino's ears the Song of the Family was as fierce as a cry. He was immune and terrible, and his song had become a battle cry. They trudged past the burned square where their house had been without even looking at it. They cleared the brush that edged the beach and picked their way down the shore towards the water. And they did not look towards Kino's broken canoe.

And when they came to the water's edge they stopped and stared out over the Gulf. And then Kino laid the rifle down, and he dug among his clothes, and then he held the great pearl in his hand. He looked into its surface and it was grey and ulcerous. Evil faces peered from it into his eyes, and he saw the light of burning. And in the surface of the pearl he saw the frantic eyes of the man in the pool. And in the surface of the pearl he saw Coyotito lying in the little cave with the top of his head shot away. And the pearl was ugly; it was grey, like a malignant growth. And Kino heard the music of the pearl, distorted and insane. Kino's hand shook a little, and he turned slowly to Juana and held the pearl out to her. She stood beside him, still holding her dead bundle over her shoulder. She looked at the pearl in his hand for a moment and then she looked into Kino's eyes and said softly : "No, you."

And Kino drew back his arm and flung the pearl with all his might. Kino and Juana watched it go, winking and glimmering under the setting sun. They saw the little splash in the distance, and they stood side by side watching the place for a long time.

And the pearl settled into the lovely green water and dropped towards the bottom. The waving branches of the algae called to it and beckoned to it. The lights on its surface were green and lovely. It settled down to the sand bottom among the fern-like plants. Above, the surface of the water was a green mirror. And the pearl lay on the floor of the sea. A crab scampering over the bottom raised a little cloud of sand, and when it settled the pearl was gone.

And the music of the pearl drifted to a whisper and disappeared.

BURNING BRIGHT

A Play in Story Form

'The story grips one, and the under-
lying idea—that we can claim no
property in anything, even in our
own children—is most effectively
dramatised.'—*Sunday Times.*

To, for,
and because of
ELAINE

CONTENTS

FOREWORD   83

ACT ONE : THE CIRCUS   87

ACT TWO : THE FARM   115

ACT THREE, SCENE I : THE SEA   139

               SCENE II : THE CHILD   153

Tyger! Tyger! burning bright
In the forests of the night,
What immortal hand or eye
Could frame thy fearful symmetry?

—WILLIAM BLAKE

FOREWORD

Burning Bright is the third attempt I have made to work in this new form—the play novelette. I don't know that anyone else has ever tried it before. Two of my previous books—*Of Mice and Men* and *The Moon Is Down*—essayed it. In a sense it is a mistake to call it a new form. Rather it is a combination of many old forms. It is a play that is easy to read or a short novel that can be played simply by lifting out the dialogue.

My reasons for wanting to write in this form are several and diverse. I find it difficult to read plays, and in this I do not find myself alone. The printed play is read almost exclusively by people closely associated with the theatre, by students of the theatre, and by the comparatively small group of readers who are passionately fond of the theatre. The first reason for this form, then, is to provide a play that will be more widely read because it is presented as ordinary fiction, which is a more familiar medium.

The second reason for the creation of the play novelette is that it augments the play for the actor, the director, and the producer, as well as the reader. The usual description of a character in a play—"Business-man, aged forty"—gives them very little to go on. It can be argued that with this terse description the burden of character portrayal must lie in the dialogue and in seeing the actor on-stage. It can further be argued that terse description gives the director and the set designer greater leeway in exercising their own imagination in production.

Against these arguments it can be said, first, that it can do no harm for theatre-goers or theatre people to have the fullest sense of the intention of the writer; and, second, that director, actor, and set designer cannot be limited, and may even be helped, by a full knowledge of the details pertinent to the action. And for the many people who have not seen the play, and will never see it, this becomes an aid to which they are entitled.

It is generally accepted that writers of regular fiction do not care, or are not able, to submit themselves to the discipline of the theatre. They do not wish to keep the action within the boundaries of the proscenium arch; they do not wish to limit themselves to curtains and to scenes projected by dialogue alone. The usual play, then, would seem to be highly confining—and so it is. There must be no entrance into thoughts of a character unless those thoughts are clearly exposed in the dialogue. People cannot wander around geographically unless the writer has provided some physical technique for making such wanderings convincing on-stage. The action must be close-built, and something must have happened to the characters when the curtain has been lowered on the final line. These working principles are applicable both to the regular play form and to the play novelette. There is one further limitation. The piece must be short.

On the rewarding side of the picture lie the concentration and discipline of the theatre and the impossibility of setting down any vagueness either intellectual or physical. You must be clear and concise. There can be no waste, no long discussion, no departure from a main theme, and little exposition. As in any good play, the action must be immediate, dynamic, and dramatic resolution must occur entirely through the characters themselves.

The difficulties of the technique are very great. The writer whose whole training has lain in the play is content to leave physical matters to his director or set designer and has not learned to use description as a fiction-writer does. On the other hand, the fiction-writer has been trained to let his description pick up his dialogue, and he tends to depart from the tight structure of the theatre. If a writer is not accustomed to *seeing* his story before his eyes, his use of this form is not likely to be successful.

Despite its difficulty, the play novelette is highly rewarding. It gives a play a wide chance of being read and a piece of fiction a chance of being played without the usual revision. I think it is a legitimate form and one that can stand a great deal of exploration.

JOHN STEINBECK

ACT ONE

THE CIRCUS

THE canvas walls of the dressing-tent were discoloured with brown water spots, with green grass stains and grey streaks of mildew, and the prickles of sun glittering came through. On the ground the close-cut barley stubble stood in bunches with the black 'dobe earth between. Near to one cloth wall there was a large and travel-beaten trunk with dull brass straps and corners, its lid upraised and a mirror the whole size of the top disclosed.

Joe Saul sat on a folding canvas chair before the trunk. He was naked to the waist, but he had on tights and slippers. He dabbed the yellow powder on his face and painted his eyes with black—not carefully.

A lithe and stringy man of middle age, Joe Saul. His jaws muscled against strain and cables down the sides of his neck. His arms were white and blue-veined, with the long cords of clinging and hanging rather than the lumps of lifting. His hands were white, the fingers spatulate, and palms and fingers calloused from the rope and bar.

Joe Saul's face was rough and a little pock-marked; his eyes looked large and dark and glittering within their pencilled edges. He finished his makeup and took a little bottle of dark hair-dye from the trunk, poured some on a brush and worked the stain into his thick, greying hair, particularly at the temples. Then neatly he packed his powder and bottles back in the trunk and slipped on the shirt of his tights and cinched his canvas belt. Only a small bulge showed over the belt. He leaned back in his chair and flexed his hands, so that the thin muscles of his forearms squirmed.

From outside the dressing-room came sounds of the developing show—call of barker and skirl of calliope and thin waltz of merry-go-round backed by the chutter of gathering people. And nearer sounded grunts of lions and whoosh of elephants, grunt and squeal of pigs and discontented snort of horses against the brass wail of a circus trombone.

And Joe Saul flexed his hands and looked down at them. From outside the flap came three short whistles in place of knocking.

"Come in," said Joe Saul, and Friend Ed stepped through the flap. Friend Ed was broader, taller, heavier than Joe Saul, slower in motion and speech. He was dressed and made up too, a big-pants clown ruffed at neck, wrists, and ankles, white suit with big red polka dots, and feet as long and curved as barrel staves : a white face, red rubber nose, sad black mouth, and black lines over the eyelids. High on his forehead were painted the inverted Vs of astonishment. He had created on his face a look of surprised perplexity. Only his thick dark hair and hands were his own. He carried the bald head with fringe of bright red hair and the big false hands.

Joe Saul closed the trunk lid to make a place for him to sit, and Friend Ed dropped his hair piece and his false hands on the trunk and seated himself on its edge and swung his big floppy clown foot gently back and forth.

"Where's Mordeen?" he asked.

"She went to sit with Mrs Malloy's baby," said Joe Saul. "Mrs Malloy's gone off to the post office to send a money order to her son, Tom," he said monotonously. "Her son Tom, '*my-son-Tom*.' He's in college, you know." Joe Saul sat up tight-straight. "I'm sure, Friend Ed, I don't tell you for the first time that Mrs Malloy has got a son Tom that's in college and only nineteen. Did you hear about that, Friend Ed? Did you hear about it twenty thousand times?"

Friend Ed opened his black mouth so that the red inner lips and little white teeth showed. "Don't curse him, Joe Saul," he said. "Or her."

"Who's cursing?" Joe Saul leaned back and flexed his

hands on his knees. "She's a nice woman," he said. "And I guess if you've got a son Tom in college you've got a little fringe of God Almighty on your head, but I wouldn't curse her. I'm glad for her. She's a nice woman."

"Now look, Joe Saul, you're nervy."

"No."

Friend Ed glanced down at the flexing hands. "That's a new thing, you're doing there. That's a nervy thing." His foot stopped its swinging.

Joe Saul looked at his hands. "I didn't know I was doing it," he said. "But you are right, Friend Ed. I've got a rustle in me. It's a little itching rustle under my skin."

"I see it coming on you, Joe Saul. It's not a thing of surprise to me except it's late. It's very late—I wonder why so late. Three years it is since Cathy died. You were strong in your wife-loss. You were not nervy then. And it's eight months since Cousin Will missed the net. You were not nervy then. Victor's a good partner, isn't he? You said he was. And it's not the first time a Saul missed the net in all the generations. What's the matter with you, Joe Saul? You're putting an itch in the air around you like a cloud of gnats in a hot evening."

Joe Saul flexed his hands, looked at them, and then he grappled them together to keep them still. "Victor's all right," he said. "Maybe better than Cousin Will. It's what you get used to. I could feel the tuning of Cousin Will. I knew his breathing and his pulse. Cousin Will was my blood and my being; we were the products of a thousand years, the end products. I have to think about Victor, think about what he'll do. I could feel Cousin Will in my nerve ends. Maybe I'll get used to Victor, but he's a stranger. His blood is not my blood. He has no ancestry in it."

Outside the tent a band struck up, playing an overture fast and hot.

"Is Mordeen made up, Joe Saul?"

"Sure. She wouldn't have gone else." His hands flexed again in spite of him, and Friend Ed noticed it.

"Is it your nerve? I've seen that happen. Do you fear for your hands? I knew a man once going blind and he ran about looking at colour, looking and staring so he'd remember. He was afraid he might forget what colour was like when he was blind. Do your hands trouble you?"

"I don't think so. Why should they? They've never slipped or lost their grip."

Friend Ed leaned over and touched Joe Saul on the shoulder. "Do I have the friend-right to ask a question, Joe Saul?"

"Always."

"Is there any trouble with Mordeen?"

"No—oh, no !"

"You're sure?"

"I'm—sure."

"It's a fine girl, Joe Saul, a fine wife. See you remember it. She's young—but very good. See you never doubt that. No man ever had better. Don't compare her with your Cathy—she's different but just as good, and lovely and true."

"I know."

"What I came to say is this. I'm having a little birthday party for the twins. They wanted only kids, but they asked for you and for Mordeen. Will you come and bring some little twist of a present?"

"Do they really ask for me?"

"They did—and will you keep your goddamned hands still?"

Joe Saul leaped up, and his slippers rustled in the stubble. He paced, holding his hands against their rest-lessness in front of him. He bit his under-lip.

Friend Ed spoke quietly. "I'll take some of the itch from you, if you'll let me. I held you weeping when your Cathy died. I lifted Cousin Will off the ring rim, and I stood left-hand to you with Mordeen. I think I know your sick-ness, but you will have to say it first, Joe Saul."

The pacing stopped. "She's taking a long time to get a

money order," he said. "I think you do know. I think your twins know. I wonder—whether Mordeen knows."

"Will you say it, then, for your mind's rest and your hands' peace? Maybe there's some kind of answer."

Joe Saul sighed. "I wonder is it age coming on me? I think of old times. They say old men think back. I think of my grandfather talking—that was after his hands were gone weak, and his timing gone and the certainty of his eye. When it didn't matter any more, he'd drink wine in the afternoon. He'd lesson us on the training-mat, and when we were resting sometimes Grandfather would talk. He did a lot of reading, that old man, and more thinking. Maybe he made up things, but we believed him. You never knew him, Friend Ed."

"No, I never knew him. Talk it out, Joe Saul! Let's find the bitter seed that's like the inside of a peach pit."

Joe Saul sat in his chair and leaned back, thinking. "We were real proud kids," he said, "with one hip up and our chests stuck out. We believed everything he said because he was Old Joe Saul. I'm named for him. He used to say that we were nature spirits once—you know, in trees and streams. We lived in the wind and in the black storms. 'That's what your great-granddads were', he'd say. Remember how white his hair was? No—you never saw him. Then he said we were the first doctors, but witch-doctors. We troubled the waters and drove the thunder back over the edge, and we jumped like the streams over rocks, and we sailed—arms out—like the wind.

"Well, then he said we were doctors against hurt, and we had to make the form of hurt and sickness to drive it out, so that we were crooked for fits and spastic for poison, and we bent like rubber for a broken leg. He had it all down, and we'd squat and listen on the training-mat." And Joe Saul squatted beside his chair to show how it was.

"It's a strange telling for children," Friend Ed interposed. "Would you some time tell it to the twins?"

"Of course I will. The twins have the blood. They'd

understand. Old Joe Saul said then in Greece we wore high shoes and wooden masks and we were gods. He said in Rome we tumbled in the red sand of the arena after the blood had run, and we juggled burning sticks in front of the set-up crosses and their burdens.

"Then in the dark centuries, he said, we laughed and played in the miracles, and we were the only gay in that laughter-starving time. From then on, he said, everybody knows."

"I'll want the twins to hear," said Friend Ed.

"I told you he'd drink a little in the afternoon when he didn't go up any more and it didn't matter. Kings, he'd say, princes, counts, Astors, Vanderbilts, or Tudors, Plantagenets, Pendragons for that matter—who knows their great-granddads with any certainty? Old Joe Saul would stand there, tall and one finger out like a dry stick. He had a full head of hair and every tooth his own. He'd stand there, a white cloud, and we were proud kids squatting on the mat, all knee and elbow burned from the workout.

" 'Two ancient families there are', he'd say, 'known and sure and recognized—and only two. Clowns and acrobats. The rest are newcomers.' "

Friend Ed breathed deep with satisfaction. "You can tell the twins at their birthday party, after the cake."

Joe Saul's face twisted with remembering now. He stood and his hands went to their gripping. "And he'd say to us: 'Have kids—have lots of kids! Be not ever without a baby on the fingers, a child on the mat, and a boy on the bar.' He'd scowl down on us sitting there."

Joe Saul was silent, and Friend Ed was silent. The sound of lightly tripping, snorting ring horses came though the tent. Friend Ed looked strongly at Joe Saul. "There's your bitter seed," he said. "There it is. Cathy had no child—but Mordeen?"

"It's been three years," Joe Saul said. "Three years."

"Do you begin to think it's you?"

"I don't know what it is—I don't know what it is. But a man can't die this way."

"Nor a woman either."

Joe Saul cried : "A man can't scrap his blood line, can't snip the thread of his immortality. There's more than just my memory. More than my training and the remembered stories of glory and the forgotten shame of failure. There's a trust imposed to hand my line over to another, to place it tenderly like a thrush's egg in my child's hand. You've given your blood line to the twins, Friend Ed. And now— three years with Mordeen."

"Maybe it's you should go to doctors. There might be a remedy you haven't thought of."

"What do they know?" Joe Saul cried. "There's some dark kind of curse on me, and I feel it."

"On you alone, Joe Saul?" Friend Ed smiled. "Do you feel singled out, pinned up alone in a museum? It's time we bring this trouble out into the air and light. Else it will grow with poisoned fingers like a cancer in your mind. Rip off the cover. Let it out! Maybe you're not alone in your secret cave."

"I know!" Joe Saul said quietly. "I guess I'm getting that way—digging like a mole into my own darkness. Of course, Friend Ed, I know it is a thing that can happen to anyone in any place and time—a farmer or a sailor, or a lineless, faceless Everyone! I know this—and maybe all of these have the secret locked up in loneliness."

"That would do it. And now that I know, I'll try to help. I'll try to think—and help."

Suddenly Joe Saul said nervously : "I wonder what's keeping Mordeen. That's a long time to get a money order. Her baby—Mrs Malloy's too old to have a baby. She's too old—she's forty-five."

"But she had it," said Friend Ed. And automatically to an unseen, unheard cue he put his hair piece on and smoothed the bald skin over his thick hair and patted the edges down on his forehead just above the incredulous eyebrows. "Now that I know, Joe Saul, I'll try to help.

I'm on——" He put on his false hands, shuffled his big feet in a mincing dance step, and flopped out of the tent.

Joe Saul lifted the lid of the trunk and pulled his little chair close and peered at himself in the mirror. He leaned close and inspected his face. Suddenly Friend Ed looked in again. "I didn't mean that—I didn't mean it that way."

"Mean what?"

"I heard it in my ears, the way it sounded when I said: 'But she had it.' I didn't mean it that way, Joe Saul."

"I didn't hear it—that way," Joe Saul said uneasily. "You're on, Friend Ed." And sure enough, the shrill band played the march of elephants and white horses, giraffes and hippopotamuses and pin-wheeling clowns. Friend Ed whirled, and the canvas dropped behind him. He called a greeting outside. "Run, Mordeen, he's waiting for you."

Now the flap lifted and Mordeen came in. Her tights were white and silver, and over her shoulders she wore a long silver and blue cape which fell in heavy folds to her ankles. Mordeen was fair and very beautiful, her golden hair in short tight curls, her eyes blued, her makeup carefully applied. She was smiling, her face alight with a pleasant memory.

Joe Saul swung round to her, his face dark and serious. "Have you seen Victor, Mordeen?"

"No, I haven't. That baby, Joe Saul, he crows, really crows, and rocks back and forth. He grabbed at a shaft of sunshine with his hand. You should have seen his face when his hand went through it, amazed and disappointed all at once." She laughed and then, seeing him and his posture: "What's the matter, Joe Saul? Aren't you well?"

"I'm all right." He stood up.

"Angry then? You must be angry. Your eyes are so black, but when you are angry they seem to have a red glow. Are you angry with me, Joe Saul?"

He moved very quickly to her and put his arms around her, and there was hunger and eagerness in his body and in his face.

"Not angry," he said. "No, not angry—and still angry."

94

He stroked her cheek. "Angry at Time when you were away. Angry at Time. Irritated with the minutes when you aren't with me."

"I like that," she said. "It's good to be missed. I came back as soon as I could. It's good to be away a little. Then I know how well and strongly I love you."

He strained her tight to him. "I get frightened," he said. "My mind plays games. It whispers that you don't exist. It sneers that you have gone away. It whines to me that there is no Mordeen. It's a cruel, mischievous game."

She was smiling and her voice was sleepy, languorous. "It's a child's game to make good things better," she said. "I remember holding a piece of white cake with black frosting and pretending it was not mine. That was to make it nicer when I tasted it. Now, Joe Saul, that's better. The red is gone out of your eyes. You have the blackest eyes—like new split coal—that black! But you were angry, or very troubled."

"If I was, I am not now," he said. "Everything bad evaporates when I touch you. I love you, Mordeen—starvingly."

"Then you are not satisfied?"

"No—never—I never am. What a dull thing that would be—like the slight, painful sluggishness of an over-full stomach, like too much food or too much sleep. No, you keep me fed and hungry, and that is the best."

She pushed him a little bit away from her so that she could look clearly into his face. "Will you tell me what is worrying you, Joe Saul?"

"It's nothing," he said.

"Is it Victor?"

"A little."

"Is it"—she paused—"anything else?"

"No—no."

"Am I a good woman to you?"

He held her tight. "Oh, my God! My God, Mordeen! You're a burning flower in my heart. See—I am harsh-breathing like a boy. I'm full of you."

95

The flap opened again and Victor entered. Joe Saul released Mordeen, slowly and proudly, and turned to face him.

Victor was large and powerful, dark and young. His mouth was full and arrogant, his eyes sullen. He wore flannel slacks and a white T-shirt, and a gold medallion on a golden chain hung at his throat. His skin bloomed with youth. He held his right arm across his stomach, and the wrist was tightly bandaged with surgical tape. He stood defiantly in the entrance. Mordeen slipped quietly round until she stood behind Joe Saul.

As for Joe Saul, he stared at Victor, first with perplexity and then with growing anger.

"Why aren't you ready?" he asked, and then he saw the tape. "What's that?"

Victor put threat and self-sufficiency on his face to cover fear. "I sprained my wrist," he said. "I just came from the doctor."

For a long moment Joe Saul regarded him and then he asked very quietly : "How?"

Victor expected anger. He was not prepared for quietness—he was not braced for quietness. He had been set and poised to repel a rage, he carried rage to defend himself. In the ominous quiet he was off balance and he could not change his pattern of defence.

"No need to get mad," he said loudly. "I couldn't help it. I tell you it was an accident. Might happen to anybody—might happen any time."

Joe Saul turned slowly back and forth like a gun-turret, and he was silent. But Victor blustered on. "I was playing, just playing around with some of the fellows—touch-football. That's all, just playing, and one guy just put out his foot—didn't mean it. Say, what's the matter with you?" He shifted back uneasily, for Joe Saul had stood up and moved slowly near to him. And Joe Saul's voice recited without rise or fall, monotonously.

"You went to high school in a little town," he said "Ohio, was it?" He did not wait for an answer. "Athlete, half mile, pole vault, tumbling team. And funny—like a clown. And everyone said that you should be on the stage, wasting your time there in the little town. Ran away with a circus—the old dream, every little boy's escape."

He stopped and licked his lips.

And Victor said : "The doctor says three days. It's only a strained tendon. What are you yelling about?"

Joe Saul went on quietly as though he had not heard. "It isn't that you didn't know, but that you can't ever know. If you were a musician, you'd bat a tennis ball with your violin. If you were a surgeon, you'd sharpen pencils with a scalpel."

Victor said : "Don't shout at me !"

Joe Saul said quietly : "It sounds like that to you, does it ? You're stronger, quicker, younger, even more sure than Cousin Will, but now I know what it is. Whatever you do is an accident of youth and muscle. You have not the infinite respect of your tools and your profession—Profession ! You have made it a trade."

Joe Saul's tone had sharpened in contempt. "And you have not even learned your trade. You did not hang clinging to your father's forefingers. You have no blood in it." He paused uneasily and looked away.

Mordeen moved closer to him, shivering a little at his quietness. And her movement caught Victor's attention and gave him his weapon. Almost with relief he put her up as a shield against the lashing.

"What's the matter—feeling old?" His eyes went to meet Mordeen.

Joe Saul asked blankly : "What?"

Victor pressed forward, like a yammering boy after a hurt cat. "What's the matter—jealous? What's the matter —afraid you can't keep up with a young girl? Is she too much for you?"

Joe Saul was staring at the ground. He sighed and he said softly : "I'll go and report that we can't go on for three days." Slowly he moved very near and struck Victor hard in the face with his open palm. Then he turned and walked lightly on his toes out of the dressing-tent.

Mordeen went quickly to the open trunk, dropped her cape over the little chair, sat down and rubbed cold cream on her face. But Victor stood in shock, unable to get over the nausea of the insult. His eyes were glazed with hatred and the inability to put it to violent use. He moved dumbly, nearer to Mordeen.

"I couldn't hit an old man, a man old enough to be my father," he said.

Mordeen rubbed the cold cream into her skin and wiped it off on a little towel. She did not look round.

"You notice I didn't raise a hand against him?" Victor said. "He knew he was safe. He knew I wouldn't hit him back—an old man like that."

"He can't hear you," Mordeen said. She wiped the eye shadow from around her eyes.

"I wouldn't care if he could. You heard me say the same thing right in his face."

"And I saw what he did to you," said Mordeen.

"I could break him with my hands," said Victor, and with his hands he showed how he could do it. "I could throw him like an old sack. Why, I could crush him—but I didn't. That wouldn't be fair."

Mordeen turned towards him. The yellow and blue and red streaked towel was in her hand. "You're really afraid of him," she said softly.

Victor surged towards her, his chest up and the muscles rippling on his shoulders. "How do you mean afraid? I tell you I could tear him apart."

Mordeen looked at him for a long minute. "Why didn't you then?" she asked.

"Because——" He fought the question because he did not know. Then he formed his answer. His voice grew silky. "Because—I'll tell you why. I have respect for you." He considered his solution. "Because I don't want trouble or fighting when there's a girl I—I am in love with."

Mordeen looked up at him in wonder. "In love with?" Her mouth stayed open after she had said it.

Victor moved closer. He put out his hand to touch her shoulder, but when she looked at his hand he took it away. "I didn't tell you," he said. "I tried to keep it in. I want to be fair. I'm not the kind of guy that creeps on his partner. But he hit me—in the face."

Mordeen said quietly: "You hit him below the belt. That's how fair you are."

Victor began: "I didn't lay a hand—oh, yes," he said, chuckling, "I see what you mean. That got him, didn't it? Next time he whips out that tongue of his, I'll get him again. I know how—now." His lips curled with hatred. He was poisoned with insult. "I don't need to hit him. I can just stand back and punish him with a word. He's old, and you can't get cured of that."

Mordeen smiled up at him. "Besides, you respect and love me," she said sardonically.

Victor shook his head, like a bruised fighter with a steady left hand in his face. And suddenly he fell back on the surest defence there is—none. It was a wrestling tactic to go limp against strain. "I'm a fool," Victor said. "Joe Saul is right. I don't know my arse from a teacup. Of course he's right. But maybe I'll learn. Maybe I'll grow up some day." His face was young and eager. "I admire Joe Saul more than anybody in the world. That's why it hurt so much when he hit me the way you'd hit a dog. That's why I hit back—because I was hurt. That's why I did it.

"Let's start fresh, Mordeen. I'll apologize to Joe Saul. He'll understand why I did it when I tell him how hurt I was. I don't know my arse from a teacup. Coming from high school, being with famous people, trying to be like them when I don't know enough. Why, it's a privilege to be taught by Joe Saul. I know it. I'm sorry I lost myself, Mordeen."

She watched him, believing and not believing, and then deciding to believe because she couldn't see what there was to lose. "I can see how that is," she said. "Oh, I've had things like that happen to me, things that made me dumb and sick. You see, Victor, we're a kind of a little world inside a world. We have a whole life and pattern most people just don't know about. Lots of people resent us or envy us. And so we're proud and maybe a little bit afraid of people. Maybe we protect ourselves too much."

"I see what you mean," he said, although he didn't at all.

"When you argue with a child," she said warmly, "you give a good argument and the child says yah, yah! You understand him and he doesn't listen, so the child wins."

"I see what you mean," he said softly. A little purr crept into his voice. She looked up for a moment in apprehension. "I see what you mean," he repeated, and the purr was gone.

He hurried on. "I never think of you growing up—here."

"But I did." Her voice was very soft. "My whole life. I was born in a sleeping-car, raised in the ring. I rode in a hoodah before I could walk."

Victor's unfortunate choice it was always to mis-see, to mis-hear, to misjudge. He read softness into her because of the softness of her voice, when she was only remembering. His was the self-centred chaos of childhood. All looks and thoughts, loves and hatreds, were directed at him. Softness was softness towards him, weakness was weakness in the face of his strength. He preheard answers and listened not. He was full coloured and brilliant—all outside of him was pale.

"You knew Joe Saul's first wife?" he said.

"Oh, yes."

"Did Joe Saul love her?"

"Oh, yes! Oh, very yes."

He paused and his lashes fell over his fine eyes. He dropped on one knee so that his eye level was a little below hers. He studied her face, or seemed to—brows, eyes, nose, upper lip well bowed, lower lip full and passionate, tight with exquisite nerves. He spoke softly but with the purr of insinuation in his voice.

"Why did you marry him?"

She raised her head, astonished. "Why?"

"Yes, why? A fifty-year-old man, or nearly, a man near-finished when you've only started. Why did you marry him?"

Mordeen smiled then with kindness at him, smiled almost with affection, as one does when a little boy first asks : "What is God?"

"I married him because—because I loved him."

"That was three years ago. Do you love him now?"

Her lips stood apart as though she listened to faintly heard music outside a summer window. "More," she said. "Much more."

He brought his malformed wisdom, his pool-hall, locker-room, joke-book wisdom to the front. "Joe Saul must be like a father in your mind," he said meanly.

"Oh, no."

He laughed. "I know more about women than you give me credit for," he said. "Isn't it true—you don't have to answer, you don't have to say anything—isn't it true that you sometimes wish for, maybe even crave, the hard arms of a young man and the smooth skin of a young man"—his voice rose—"the force, and body lust, and crushing passion of a young man?"

"No," she said softly. "That is not true. That is not true."

"I don't believe you," he said. "I know more than that."

Her kindness towards him lasted on as though there were enough warm blanket over her life so that she could spare a corner for his shoulders.

"I guess you really don't believe me," she said. "Maybe that will be your sorrow. Maybe some time in a cold perplexity you'll wonder what you missed, and maybe you'll only be dimly aware of missing something."

"I'm not a baby," he cried. "I've been around. I've known women."

"Happy women?"

"When I got through with them they were happy."

"For how long?"

He boasted: "They weren't happy until they could have me again. They always wanted me again."

"Of course. And they'll be wondering what they missed. I'm not telling any secret—Joe Saul knows that I had some other life. I know the tricks, techniques of duration, of position, games, perverse games to drive the nerves into a kind of hysterical laughter."

Victor's mouth was wet now, and he breathed through his mouth and his tongue went over his lips. "I told you I didn't believe you."

She said: "Joe Saul knows one trick, one ingredient. You haven't heard about it. Maybe you never will. Without that trick you'll one day go screaming silently in loss. Without it there are no good methods or techniques. You know, I've wondered how it is that one act can be ugly and mean and enervating, like a punishing drug, and also most beautiful and filled with energy, like milk."

Victor stood up and he spoke with uneasy truculence. "What is this trick that makes a young girl fall in love with Old Joe Saul? Do you think he can do anything I can't do?"

"Yes."

"What is this ingredient?"

"Affection," she said softly. "You have never learned it. Very many people never do."

Victor was uneasy, and he felt failure—that he had been caught in a failure. He said loudly: "You mean I'm not as good a man as Old Joe Saul? Let me try, and I swear to God you'll never go back to him. Ah! we're all alike, men, women. What are you telling me? A jump in the hay is a jump in the hay. What's this breathless thing?"

"All alike," she said. "Surely—all alike. And everyone who hammers out a tune makes music, and when one rough line rhymes with another that's great poetry, and every daub on canvas is a great painting."

"What are you getting at?" he asked uneasily.

Mordeen said: "I used to wonder why this love seemed sweeter than I had ever known, better than many people ever know. And then one day the reason came to me. There are very few great Anythings in the world. In work and art and emotion—the great is very rare. And I have one of the great and beautiful. Now say your yah, yah, Victor, like a child unanswerably answering Wisdom. You will have to do that, I think."

Victor said: "If it's so goddamn good, why does he have the jerks? Why does he go stepping around like a cat on hot bricks? Why's his temper short and the grey coming into his sick face? Tell me that if it's so goddamn good."

Mordeen had become rigid, her mouth tight and her eyes veiled.

"You do have a gift," she said. "Instinctively you know where to put the knife and how to twist it. I know what you mean, but you don't know. You groped blindly and found a thing as precious as a porcelain door-knob in the dark." She stood up and stepped close to him. Her face was cold and her voice icy. "I want to tell you this," she said. "Maybe I'm telling myself. I will do anything—anything—anything to bring content to him. See you remember that, Victor."

His guard was up now and he wasn't listening; he was only angry because here was a world he could not enter and so he had to disbelieve in its existence. He fell back on the world he knew. He said: "You're setting yourself high. What makes you so special?"

"Joe Saul," she said quickly.

"You're a woman like any other woman—same equipment, no more, no less. Everything else is the same too. You need what every girl in the world needs—a little bit of forcing so you can claim it wasn't your fault. Maybe you need the back of the hand, maybe you need——" He grabbed her in his arms, holding her elbows against her sides. "Maybe you need—me." He leaned over to kiss her and she sagged and relaxed so that, holding her, he could not reach her mouth with his mouth. Her head fell limply away from him and her body hung dead in his arms.

Victor was puzzled now. He had instinctively pinned her arms against resistance. Her eyes were closed, and she was still. Outside the tent-flap there were three short whistles instead of knocking. But neither Victor nor Mordeen heard. The whistles were repeated, and then Friend Ed stepped through the flap. His makeup was off, but he still wore his polka-dot clown suit. He stood looking at Victor's back. Then slowly he moved towards them.

Victor was worried. "Mordeen," he said, "Mordeen, are you all right?" He released his arms, and as he did, she stepped quickly back away from him. Her face was snarling with hatred and contempt. Then she saw Friend Ed and she stared at him.

Victor looked round and his hand went up protectively. Friend Ed stepped closer. "Go away," he said softly. "Go away now! I'll never tell. I think Joe Saul would kill you."

Victor said : "I didn't——"

"Go away. It wouldn't be good for Joe Saul to kill you —not good for Joe Saul. Even if they didn't catch him, he'd carry a sourness all his life. You're not worth that much to him or to me. Tell him you have to leave the show—your mother died, anything. But go!"

"I—you don't know——"

Friend Ed dropped his shoulders and moved closer. "Maybe I'll have to take the sourness myself. Please, please go away!"

Victor said : "Nobody can make me go away." He looked at his taped wrist. "You watch yourself."

"All right, but go away now, go away."

Victor hesitated. "Don't think I'm afraid," he said, but he walked to the flap and disappeared.

Mordeen and Friend Ed watched him go and then they

turned sluggishly and looked at each other, and they seemed to look through cloudy water so that they had to stare to see at all. A wall of slowness separated them.

Mordeen said in a dreaming voice: "You saw all that, Friend Ed?"

"Yes, I saw."

"What do you believe?"

"I believe what I saw."

"Do you think Joe Saul would?"

"He would want to—he would have to, and if he couldn't I would try to make him."

Mordeen sighed deeply. She said: "Victor knowing nothing and feeling very little has an instinct for finding frail places and areas of pain. I'm sure he doesn't know anything, and still he feels and probes like a blind leech and he gets blood."

Friend Ed looked at her for a long moment. "Joe Saul reported the act couldn't·go on and then he went to a bar. He's getting drunk, Mordeen."

She sat down wearily, started to speak. "I must——" and she was silent.

"Do you want to talk to me?" Friend Ed asked.

"Yes—yes, I do. There's a cloud coming down. I want to talk. He's getting drunk. Is that part of the cloud?"

"Do you know what the cloud is?"

"Yes. Do you?"

"Yes."

Friend Ed asked quickly: "Will you tell me this: can you have a baby?"

Mordeen looked away from him. "Yes, I can."

"How do you know?"

"The only way I could know. I know."

"When did it happen?"

"Five years ago."

"Does Joe Saul know?"

"No, he doesn't. It was before. It was all dead and done, before Joe Saul."

Friend Ed said: "I don't understand it. He hasn't

105

never been sick that I know of. He's a twisting mass of strength and force."

She said softly: "He was sick once. He told me. It was the only time and when he was a boy. Growing pains, they called it. His bones and his joints ached and the fever burned him. For a year he was whipped with pain."

Friend Ed's eyebrows rose. "And you took his account and discovered——"

"Yes, rheumatic fever."

"And could that be the cause?"

"Yes," she said. "It could. It need not but it could." She said passionately: "Can't we tell him? Could we bring this in the open? We need a baby. We can get one, adopt it, and it will be ours. Maybe if this thing were certain and understood the cloud would go away. Maybe——"

"I don't think you can tell him that," Friend Ed said. "I don't think that would be good. Do you know what happens to a man when he knows he is sterile?"

"I know he is miserable now and hungry, starving for a child. I know it has always been, but now it's frantic."

"Is he a good lover?"

"Oh, wonderful! Gentle and fierce and—wonderful."

Friend Ed said quietly: "When the bodies of man and woman meet in love there is a promise—sometimes so deep buried in their cells that thinking does not comprehend—there is a sharp promise that a child may be the result of this earthquake and this lightning. This each body promises the other. But if one or the other knows—knows beyond doubt that the promise can't be kept—the wholeness is not there; the thing is an act, a pretence, a lie, and deeply deep, a uselessness, a thing of no meaning."

"I know," she said.

"How it is with a woman I'm not sure," he continued. "But with a man—perhaps he may feel free because he is in no danger; and perhaps the woman may feel wildly free in lust without consequence, but in her tissues there is contempt for a sterile man. And in a man there is a searching for the contempt he knows is there. Then, no matter how she pretends and protests and covers the sadness of the sterile love, he knows and feels it. And since we do not willingly do futile things, the man's body gradually refuses to perform a useless act, and the woman—oh, very slowly—has no need for him and her senses turn away from the dark double disappointment."

Mordeen looked down at her hands and she said: "I don't think that is so with me. I think I would do anything —anything my mind or heart or body can conceive—to give contentment to Joe Saul."

Friend Ed replied: "That is because he does not know. Once he knows—knows beyond every hiding, boding doubt that his seed is dead—he will not permit you even to try. The fog of his self-contempt will settle over him, and you will not be able ever to find him again in his grey misery."

"Then what should I do?" she asked.

"I don't know," he said. "It would be different if his mind and energy could rove creatively in the stars of mathematics or build out of eight notes a pattern of music new and living—then he might survive. But these things he does not have, and most men do not. Swinging on his high bar, timing his swing to catch your turning body—this is as old and instinctive to him as chewing when meat is in his mouth."

"What shall I do?"

"Don't make him know."

"But suppose it is not true. Suppose by some accident he becomes alive; suppose the fault is mine, an organ disarranged, an acid improperly applied by my own body, a poisoned thought lying concealed but toxic."

"You don't believe that," Friend Ed said. "I know you. You've had all the tests. You know."

She put her forehead in her hands. "Do you know how I love this man, Friend Ed?"

"I think I do. I hope I do."

107

"Do you know I would protect him from hurt if I were ripped and burned in the process?"

"That would be only a double burning."

"Do you know I am capable of any lie or cheat or violence—any good or bad that a human can conceive—for his content and joy?"

"I think you are. And I wonder what tiny mote of chance there is of its succeeding."

She looked at him closely. "You know what I am considering, don't you?"

"I think so."

"If I were very careful, took every precaution, don't you think there is a possibility?"

"I can't advise you. I don't know."

"But without it what chance is there?"

"I don't know. I will not advise you. I might be wrong."

"But of only two choices and both wrong, and one long waiting and it wrong too—must I not choose the least wrong of three?"

Friend Ed beat his hands together. "I don't know. I tell you I will not advise you. I will not offer my responsibility, I will not endorse your note of happiness. Anything, anything else. I wish I didn't know, I wish I did not even a thread suspect what you are thinking and planning."

Mordeen sat very straight. "I know you are his friend," she said. "I suppose I put too much burden on friendship. It isn't a rope that can take that much strain. I should have made the pattern by myself, Friend Ed. But I was lonely and unsure. I thought I needed some strength outside myself to help me. I'm sorry."

"Then you will——"

"Hush," she said softly. "I will close everything away in a dark self. If I am wrong about anything it will be *my* wrongness, and you need not think it or touch it."

He bowed his head.

Mordeen said: "He would not like me to see him drunk, particularly if his drinking is not happy. Find him, Friend Ed, stay with him. And when he is tired beyond wakefulness, take him to the sleeping-car and cover him well. See his clothes are off. You'll find his night things in the black case under the lower berth—and wind his watch —and see his chest is covered when he sleeps."

"You?" he asked.

"Oh, yes—tell him I had a little headache and I will walk for a while. Tell him I will come to him very soon."

"I'm afraid," he said.

"I was. I was more afraid than I have ever been in a small, terrified life. But now I am not. Maybe I needed your weakness to build my own strength. He might be in need. Hurry, Friend Ed. Change your clothes quickly and find him. Put him to sleep before the night show. Do this for us." She took him by the arm and led him to the flap and held it back for him. And Friend Ed went uncertainly away.

Then quickly she came back and leaned over the mirror in the trunk lid and brushed her short hair. She was putting on her lipstick when the flap opened and Victor stepped quietly in. Victor wore slacks and a bright shirt, a sports coat, and a painted tie. His shoes were white and brown. Across his tie hung a gold chain from which a small gold football dangled. She saw him in the mirror of her trunk. She turned halfway towards him and spoke in flat, quick voice : "Why did you come back?"

He said sullenly : "Did you think I could be frightened away? No, I want to square things off. I followed Joe Saul into town and then came back. I waited for that one to go. I want to square some things away with you."

She made a great effort. "I'm sorry and ashamed, Victor. I was going to try to find you—to say I'm sorry."

He scowled at her. "What changed you then? Have a fight with your old man? He's getting drunk, you know— or did you know?—pig-drunk. I stood beside him in the bar, and he looked at me with juicy red eyes and he didn't even know me—that happy man, that good old lover with his trick."

"I'm sorry, Victor, really sorry."

"What changed you then?" he asked. "Did you suddenly find out that maybe I was right, that maybe this soggy stuff you thought was love might be a wizened imitation?"

"No, not quite that," she said.

"Or did you dig down through your pile of sticky words and find out that they were only words, when you needed hard and young action?"

"No, not quite that," she said.

"I came in to tell you once and finally what I think of the crap you were shovelling around. I want you to know that I won't have any of it. You were pretty tough, pretty sure. You know, you sit on the very peak top of the dung-hill and look down on all the other chickens. You're perfect, and me, I—I'm filth. Well, I tell you, I'm only honest. I'm not caught up in your stinking cloud." He paused and then continued : "And I don't believe you are either."

She said : "I was going to try to find you and tell you I was sorry."

"Why should you be sorry? What do you want of me?"

"After you left, I knew you were hurt," she said. "I told you how tight and clannish we are in this business. I'm afraid we have a way of rejecting everyone who was not born in it and descended from parents and grandparents who were born in it."

"You sure made me feel welcome!" he said sneeringly, and his eyes were very hostile.

"That's what I thought about," she said. "You are in our profession. If you stay you will have children born to it. We—I should not have cut you off the way I did. An act like ours is a kind of family, Victor. We—I should have made you feel more part of us."

"It's too late now. Your old man hit me in the face and you played dead, and the goddamned clown—did you hear what he said to me? Does he think I'll run away?"

"He didn't understand," she said. "Maybe we're so

close-clotted that none of us understood. I'd like to make you feel welcome."

"How are you going to go about that?" he said.

"I don't know," she said. "If we have hurt you so deeply, I don't know. I thought of a possible way, but I don't know."

He eyed her foxily and a secret triumph began to creep over him. He said vulgarly: "Well, I know one way you could make a start."

Her eyes were wide on him. "I would like to be friends with you, Victor. I mean that. And maybe the others—maybe I can help to make you welcome."

He came close to her. "I guess I don't care so much about the others."

"Yes, you do. I think you do. Victor, I thought of something. When I was a little girl I had a time of sharp loneliness. I guess everyone has. I felt unwanted and cold, rejected. I took all the pennies I had and bought presents and wrapped them and gave them to myself. I thought that if the other children saw how I got presents they would know I was very popular and they would want to be my friends. But it didn't work. And then, Victor, an older girl got into trouble. She stole a ring. She was afraid and she was wary of the friends she had. She came to me for help, and I helped her, and—listen, Victor—I felt warm and wanted. I felt good when I could give something so frantically needed, and I was not lonely any more."

He said: "You're funny. You always tell stories. What's this one about? What do you want me to get from it? Your stories are loaded, Mordeen." But his voice had lost its sullenness. And he smiled a little in spite of himself. "Tell me," he said. "What's your story about?"

"Well," she began hesitantly, "it is about making you feel welcome. And I thought that if you would help me, when I need help, it might be a good rich thing for both of us."

His truculence was going out of him and in spite of himself a jauntiness crept in. "Now who would think you needed help?" he said. "I thought I was the one needed help. That's what you said."

"Victor, you saw yourself that there is a trouble on us. Maybe if I could explain it so that you could understand it, you might be willing to help me." Her eyes appealed to him, and Victor went past understanding, went into triumph. He put his hand out to touch her shoulder—withdrew it when her shoulder moved imperceptibly away. Suddenly he laughed and his hand settled with authority on her shoulder.

"Why, I'd do anything for you, baby," he said. And then : "I'm sorry I was rough with you before. I know better than that. I guess I was afraid of you. I've got over that now." He stared at her. "Maybe you've changed. But they say women and horses know when a man isn't sure of himself. They can tell, no matter how much he bluffs."

Mordeen's eyes veiled with pain, and she withdrew a little into herself. "I thought you might understand," she said softly.

"I do," he cried. "Christ, what a fool a man can be ! I hear the signals, I see the lights, and I'm just dumb. I know a dame can't make the first move. How stupid can I be? Here you've thought it over, and I'm dragging my toe like a country boy."

He laughed again. "Let's get the hell out of here. Your old man's drunk. We'll go to a show. We'll go to town and have dinner. Say, how would it be if I rent a car and we go for a ride?"

Her face had tightened now. She turned away from him towards the trunk. She picked up a lipstick and drew on full lips. Her throat was tight, but she had made her decision. Her haggard face smoothed out and imperceptibly her posture became soft and provocative.

"How about it?" he demanded.

When she turned to him again she was different.

"How about what, Victor?" she said huskily.

"How about dinner and we go for a ride?"

She looked up at him, studying his face. "That will be very nice," she said. Her intonation had changed. "I don't get out very much." She continued to stare at him.

"What do you see?" he asked gaily.

"See? Oh, I was noticing how black your eyes are."

"Don't you like them?"

"Oh yes. I was thinking how some families have a black-eyed child and a blue-eyed child. It's strange."

"Not in my family," he crowed. "There hasn't been a light one on either side that anyone knows."

"That's strange," she said. "Families have such strange qualities. I knew a family that had fits and, do you know, in every second generation there was insanity."

"You know funny people. I guess we're lucky. Old age is the only thing that can kill us. My grandparents, all four, are still alive, and my great-grandfather on my father's side knocked off at a hundred and four. No, we're tough. But what are we doing here? Let's get the hell out of here."

"Yes," she said, "that will be nice." She stood up and pulled her long cape over her shoulders. "I'll go back to the sleeping-car and dress," she said. "I'll have to look nice. We'd better not be seen. Where can I meet you?"

He studied her. "No," he said slowly, "I guess you won't stand me up. Baby, there's a Chinese joint—nice booths. It's on Twelfth Street, but round the corner from the bank. It's like in an alley. I'll be in the first booth with the curtains drawn." He smiled down on her, flashing. "I'll take care of you, honey. I won't get you into any trouble. You just trust me."

She stood up and moved towards the flap. "Don't come out with me. I'll meet you in an hour." She stopped, and the spirit almost left her.

Victor stood beside her and he felt the change. He slipped his arm cosily about her waist. "I bet I know what you're thinking," he said. "Don't worry about it. We didn't invent this—it happens every day. It's nobody's fault. Don't you feel bad. Why, it can happen to anybody! We aren't so special. It can happen to anybody."

"Don't come out with me," she said.

She went out and left him. And almost instantly she was back. "He's coming. I saw him coming. Quick, get out! Quick!"

He went to the other side of the tent, lifted the canvas from the ground, and slipped underneath.

Mordeen breathed deeply. She parted the flap and looked out. She seemed about to go and then withdrew. But the next moment she was gone—gone in a flash.

The light was golden and soft now. The afternoon slid down the tent. From outside, the circus band struck up the recessional march, and below the music there was the thud of elephants' feet and the whinnying of horses. A lion roared in hunger, and suddenly a whole family of pigs went squealing.

Then the tent flap opened and Joe Saul looked in. His eyes rolled vacantly and his mouth was wet and loose. His shoulders hung askew and his tie was crooked in his unbuttoned shirt collar.

"Mordeen," he said thickly. "Mordeen, I'm drunk. I'm sorry, but I'm drunk." He peered at the trunk standing open. He staggered to the little chair and sat down. His hand fluttered lovingly over the trunk. He picked up her lipstick, smelled it, and he smiled. Clumsily he put the trunk in order and patted the tray that held the powder and grease-paint and cold cream. He caught sight of himself in the mirror and stared at his loose, drunken face. Then suddenly he slammed the trunk lid shut. The tinkle of broken mirror sounded through its sides. He put his head down on his arm, cradled his face against his forearm. His right fist struck the trunk top hard, then more softly. "Mordeen," he said, "I hurt Friend Ed. Sent him away." His fist fell and the fingers slowly opened.

Friend Ed looked in at the flap. He saw Joe Saul, watched him a moment, and then entered silently. Friend Ed squatted down on the ground and crossed his ankles. He crossed his arms lightly and took up his vigil over Joe Saul.

ACT TWO

THE FARM

THE June morning sun peered over the ridge-pole of the barn and fell across the farmhouse porch and tumbled bright and yellow through the windows into the kitchen. The light reflected from the polished metal of the stove and glittered on the pie tins set up in the warmer to dry. It was a kitchen to live in : a square table covered with oil-cloth, for eating and figuring and sewing and reading; straight chairs with little pads in their seats for comfort; a big calendar from an implement house, but a calendar for keeping notes, with room around the dates to fill in plans projected for seeding and cultivating and harvesting. It was a self-sufficient kitchen. There was even a cot under the window where a tiring wife might rest while the bread was baking. On a shelf beside the sink stood a little radio playing the sprightly music of the morning, a record of a circus band playing a wild recessional.

This was a warm and old and comfortable kitchen, beaten into ease by generations. From outside came the farmyard noises of chickens cackling, of pigs grunting, of horses snorting and whinnying in their stalls. And a late rooster crowed as though he could not give up his morning song even though the sun was risen. A tea-kettle hummed steam on the stove, a coffee-pot grunted and bumped beside it. The farm clock ticked, its pendulum flashing by the little glass window.

Joe Saul, the farmer, sat by the table, his head down on his elbow. His right hand held a pen, and in front of him was an open ink bottle. Friend Ed, who owned a neighbouring farm, sat hunched down in a chair beside him. Both men were dressed in blue jeans and blue shirts open at the throat. Their coffee-cups stood on the table in front of them.

Friend Ed got up and took his coffee-cup to the stove and filled it. "Want a refill?" he asked.

Joe Saul raised his head and shoved his coffee-cup over to the edge of the table. "Thanks," he said.

Friend Ed filled his cup. "You ought to get a book-keeper to do it for you. That's what I do. There's getting to be so much paper-work a man hasn't time to bring in a crop."

Joe Saul sipped his coffee, then added sugar and cream. "When I can't keep books on my own farm I ought to give up farming," he said. "I've always been good at arithmetic, but there's just too much of it. But it's not only that. I've got to do everything myself—or at least be there."

"Isn't Victor working out?" Friend Ed asked.

"Oh, he's a good enough worker—tries anyway. But he's got no blood for it, Friend Ed. Before Cousin Will was killed I could send him out to cultivate and know and be sure it would be done right. But Victor's a town boy. Sometimes he does things right, but you can't be sure. I have to be with him all the time. You know how it is, Friend Ed, with you and me, and how it was with Cousin Will and our fathers and grand- and great- and great-great-grandfathers—we do things, and we don't know how or why, but it's right. You can't be told about the land or read about it. It's got to be in the blood. I'm not criticizing Victor : he tries hard and mostly he's all right, but I just can't be sure. I've always got to go and look."

"I know," Friend Ed observed. "A funny thing happened like that with the twins. Al said at breakfast yesterday : 'I've got a feeling about something I should do.'

And Eddie said : 'I know. Your green beans want poles.' Just like that, as if the green beans were calling to him."

"That's what I mean," Joe Saul said. "They've got the blood. You'd never have to look at a patch of corn if the twins did the hoeing. Oh, my God almighty!"

"Now stop this," Friend Ed said. "Now stop this! You're tearing yourself like a rupture."

Joe Saul said : "I get a nightmare sometimes. I see this land—this sweet flat black land—and in my nightmare it goes back to fallow, and then the sumac comes back in clumps, and then the forest trees, and this house moulders away until there's only a chimney and cellar-hole. The farm goes back the way it was when Old Joe Saul pulled up and took salt and pepper and tobacco, gunpowder and seed corn, from his saddle-bags. That's all he had, Friend Ed, those and an axe. He cut five trees and planted his seed corn with a pointed stick. He used to tell about it when we were little kids tending our first calves." He gestured towards the door with his hand. "And look at it now—flat and black and sweet, shining like steel when the spring plough cuts in. And in ten years it could be nearly the way it was, with no one to keep it up. I get nightmares, too, of strangers—maybe from the towns, who don't know how to drain and damp."

"Stop it, Joe Saul. You worry at yourself like a puppy with a pig's ear. Get back to your paper-work and stop mauling yourself. How's Mordeen?"

"Well, I don't know. She's a little sickly the last two weeks. There's one thing worries me, Friend Ed. She's had an ache or two before and you'd never know it. She's farm stock—get up and do her work and never a complaint or a shirk in her. And now—well, her stomach *is* upset, sure, and she's a little dizzy sometimes, but she's different. She went to the doctor yesterday. She says he told her it was nothing serious, but she'd have to take it easy. It's funny. She's almost lah de dah! This morning she said : 'Would you mind if I didn't get up for a while, I don't feel quite well.' Now you know that's not like her.

And then she stretched her arms and got a funny little smile. Didn't look sick at all, but her stomach *is* upset."

"She'll be all right," Friend Ed said quietly. "Women go through queer times." And he changed the subject. "One thing I've been meaning to ask you. Does Victor seem to hold a grudge for that bawling out you gave him?"

"Why, no. I don't think so. He's pretty quiet, doesn't talk much. Seems to go about his business and do his work. I think it did him good maybe."

"I was a little worried," said Friend Ed. "I thought maybe you shouldn't have hit him."

"I'm sorry about that," Joe Saul said. "I lost my temper. I told him I was sorry. I think he's forgot it."

"It wasn't like you to hit him or any man, Joe Saul."

"He said a thing. He said a thing that made me red mad. Do you hear Mordeen stirring around? I thought I heard her."

"I guess she's up," said Friend Ed. "I should be going. With all the work I've got to do on my place, I sit round in your kitchen after sun-up. Is your clock right?"

"Set it with the radio—it's always right."

A record started softly on the radio, a wailing torch song.

Joe Saul looked over at it. "I don't know how we managed before we had it. We hardly ever turn it off. It's like another person in the house. And Mordeen listens while she does her work." He sighed. "Let's have a fresh cup of coffee. Here, give me your cup. I'll wash it out."

He carried the cups to the sink and rinsed them.

The door opened and Mordeen came in. Her face was blooming and there was a small, satisfied smile on her mouth. She wore a quilted flowered dressing-gown which reached almost to the floor.

Both men looked at her, and Joe Saul said: "Feeling better, Mordeen?"

"Oh, yes. Yes, much better."

Friend Ed said: "You look fine to me."

She moved to the couch under the window and sat down on it. "How beautiful a day," she said in wonder, as though it were the first day in the world.

"It's growing weather," Joe Saul said. "Shall I get you a little breakfast? There's oatmeal and crisp bacon in the warmer."

"You cook for me?" She laughed a low, happy laugh. "I should have got your breakfast. But it's nice to hear your offer, Joe Saul, it's very nice. No, I don't want breakfast."

"Coffee, then? I'm just going to empty the pot and make a fresh one. Would you like some nice fresh coffee?"

"No," she said. "But I'm not really sick. I think I'm just indulging myself."

"It will be the first time," Joe Saul said. "It's a new thing with you."

She drew a deep breath, started to speak. "I——"

"Yes?" Joe Saul asked.

"I don't know what I started to say. My mind went flying off."

Joe Saul carried the filled cups of coffee to the table. "If you aren't going to have some, I won't make another pot, but maybe, if you don't feel well, I'd better. Victor will be in for his mid-morning coffee soon."

Mordeen moved slowly in on what she had to say. She smiled to herself, and then her face was serious, and then she smiled again. She looked down at her hands, palm upward on her lap, one holding one, and the fingers relaxed and like a nest. "The doctor told me to take it very easy for a while," she said.

Joe Saul put down his cup and looked at her, twisting his chair round. "But he said you were all right. What does he think is the matter?"

And now she said it straight and clearly. "Joe Saul, I'm going to have a baby—*we're going to have a baby.*"

He did not hear at first because he had not been listening for it, but the words repeated themselves silently in his ears. His face set, looking at her, and the words repeated themselves again deep in his brain. For a moment Joe Saul fought his trembling chin. And then he put his head down on his arms and wept.

Friend Ed was looking at Mordeen, looking closely.

She looked back and her face was grave. She nodded. And then she smiled again.

An earthquake of emotion shook Joe Saul. Friend Ed looked away from him. But Mordeen smiled inwardly, watching her hands loving each other in her lap. Her face was withdrawn in mystery. The secrets of her body were in her eyes—the zygote new thing in the world, a new world but formed of remembered materials : the blasto-derm, the wildly splitting cells, and folds and nodes, the semblance of a thing, projections to be arms and legs and vague rays of ganglia, gill slits on the forming head, pro-jections to be fingers and two capacities from which to see one day, and then, a little man, whole formed, no bigger than the stub of a pencil and bathed in warm liquor, drawing food from the mother bank and growing. This frantic beingness lay under her loving hands embraced in a slow ecstasy in her lap.

And then Joe Saul stood up and walked heavily on his heels to the window and he looked out on his farm. He grasped his arms behind his back and pulled his shoulders up.

"Now," he said, "now it's all right." He raised his voice as though he called to the land. "Now it's all right." He laughed and turned his fierce delighted face back to the room. He released his arms and patted his hips gently as he spoke. "I've heard that in some parts of Europe they go out to the barns and tell the cattle. Why, every form is good and every ceremony." And he said : "Now that the black is lifted I can speak of blackness. So many of us nested in this land that we were it and it was part of us, so that the spring grass grew out of our pores and the green daggers of the corn came sprouting from our stom-achs. You know, Friend Ed, how the unseasonable drought is like a dryness in the chest and how unplanned heat is a fever in us." He went on softly : "The generations of us—a totem, man on man, back to the first man—and the plans for future men and future great-grand men—all lying orderly in the blueprint chromosomes."

Friend Ed smiled. "I think you might like to give a party. I'll bring the twins. I'll get ice-cream and whisky and I'll kill a turkey. This is a moment of great joy, Joe Saul. And where did I hear that?"

Joe Saul said : "Now that the black is up I can speak of black, but I can't remember it very well. I can't remember how it felt now the triumph is in me." He went to Friend Ed. "I see myself and myself's torment whirling away out of range of sight and feeling—torment in blood and heart that the line, a preciousness carried and shielded through the stormy millennia, is snapped, the product discontinued, the stamen mildewed."

"It's all over, Joe Saul. Would you like to invite some friends? Does Mordeen want it known so soon?"

They looked at her, and Friend Ed said more loudly to catch her attention : "Mordeen, do you want it known?"

She smiled. "Oh, yes. Why should I not? What is the matter, Joe Saul? Aren't you glad?"

"Glad? Oh, yes. But remembering—remembering the pain—it's like looking last in a coffin—there it is. The face is dead and you can't forget it. But if you do not look, the face is never dead and you cannot in your back mind say goodbye. And so I am looking back at the sadness so deep dug in. The top mind denies sterility. I remember how it was. Being convinced, I denied the desolation or made a joke of it—a bitter joke. I can remember only vaguely now the slow suspicious hatred that can grow and flower between man and woman while they say : 'Not now. We can't afford a child. We don't want a child if we can't take perfect care of it.' Or they say : 'We have great things to do in the world—great work that would be inhibited by a child. Our time is too precious for the squalling and noise and mess and—the expense.' "

"Would a party tire you, Mordeen?" Friend Ed asked. "Don't you think we should have a laughing party?"

"I do," she said. "I want a great scrabbling party full of noise, violent and crazy. That's what I want, Joe Saul. Come from your blackness now, Joe Saul."

"It's going fast," he said. "It's like a wound that, healing, leaves no memory, but only a scar of insensitive skin. Only the fecund can mention sterility at all. The sterile feel in their guts the desolate secret knife. Only the sterile really know through default the great two laws, that one must live and one must pass that life along—carry the fire and pass it down. The blood must flow, and the genes are ordered to communicate." He paused and shook his head violently.

Victor came up on the porch and entered the kitchen. He wore overalls and an open blue shirt. His arms were brown. "I thought I'd come in for a cup of coffee," he said. He caught some feeling from the room and was silent.

Joe Saul moved to Mordeen and looked at her as though she were new and unknown in his eyes. And she raised her head and her eyes brushed over Victor for a moment and then rose to face Joe Saul.

He said "Mordeen" softly, experimentally, as though he had never pronounced this name before. There was a wonder in his eyes. He sighed the great shuddering sigh that follows active love. He said: "Mordeen, we have a child," not telling her but tasting the words.

Victor's head snapped up. "What did you say?"

Then Joe Saul whirled on him. "You heard. We have a child," he shouted. "There's going to be a baby playing in this house. There's going to be a child playing in that dust. There's going to be a growing thing discovering the sky and kicking the chickens aside and finding eggs!" Joe Saul's body wove from side to side. He laughed hysterically in a surge of great joy. "There'll be great questions asked and answered. Do you understand that? We will rediscover the whole world. Can you hear that? This land will have its own plant growing out of it—born to it, knowing it."

His voice grew soft, almost whispered, and his eyes saw. "Our child will lie chest-flat, cheek-flat, against the ground. His toes will kick the dirt and his ear will listen and the earth will speak to him."

Victor smiled, a tight, concealing smile, and his eyes met Joe Saul's and then passed on to Mordeen, and his smile deepened. "Congratulations, Joe Saul," he said. "This calls for celebration. But you say 'he'. How do you know it will be a boy?"

Joe Saul shouted: "How do I know? What do I care? I am not dead. My blood is not cut off. My immortality is preserved. I am not dead! Boy? Girl? There will be more —and boys or girls." He went close and pounded his fist gently on Victor's chest, forcing him back a little. "We have got a child," he said. "It's right there growing. It came from me—do you hear? It came from me. And it will be a piece of me, and more, of all I came from—the blood stream, the pattern of me, of us, like a shining filament of spider silk hanging down from the incredible ages."

Joe Saul sat down, exhausted. But in a moment he threw back his head and laughed.

Then Joe Saul rose up, prancing like a heavy horse, dancing unguilefully, and laughing too. He waltzed, his arms held out as though he balanced a partner; heavy-footed he was, and his knees were bent. And the little radio played the waltz for him. And he was silly, as a joy-stuffed child is silly. Mordeen watched him, smiling, and Victor's eyes followed him, and Victor went disgustedly to fill the coffee-pot. Friend Ed laughed at his antic clumsiness.

"I never have seen you this way, Joe Saul," he cried.

"I never had reason," said Joe Saul, and he stopped in his dancing.

"Well, reason or none, I have chores to do. They don't understand reasons—good or bad."

Joe Saul drew himself up in towering mock-majesty.

"I here declare a holiday, a holy day," he orated. "I here declare that chores do not exist. Let your twins do them, or let them not be done. Argue with me, and I will flick my hand—like this—and your farm will disappear." He laughed at his own funniness. "Give me more argument, and I will flick twice—like this—and you will disappear." He whirled. "Victor, in the cabinet—get the whisky—get glasses. You want a party—it begins now. This empress"—he bowed towards Mordeen and, looking at her, his throat closed and the play went nearly out of him—"this queen, this mother wants a party. She has it. Hurry, Victor, before the party gets away," and Joe Saul ran to help to bring the glasses. He poured large portions.

Mordeen said : "None for me. I'd like it but I can't. I'll have to leave such things for a while."

In the middle of his gaiety Joe Saul became stone. He walked to the cot where she sat. He kneeled in front of her and put his hands on her knees. "Take care," he said. "Walk tenderly. Oh, take gentle care. Rest, and let your thoughts be high and beautiful." And he added hoarsely : "I order you to lift no burden, to encourage no weariness. You are to call me—me—when any work heavy or hard or long or even tiresome is to be done. Do you hear me? I order this."

She put her hand on his head affectionately and moved her fingers in his hair. "I will obey you," she said. "And it's a pleasant thing. I will take care. But I'm not as delicate as you think. There's a frightening endurance in expectant women. I will obey. Now have your drink." She put her hands under his elbows and raised him to his feet. "Drink ! Begin your party."

His mood changed then. He stepped to the table and raised his glass. "To the Child !" he shouted, and he drained his glass, and Friend Ed and Victor drank after him.

Quickly he filled the glasses. And Friend Ed raised his glass high. "To the Mother," he cried.

They drank again. "That's good," Joe Saul said. "That's the one I should have said first. That's good, Friend Ed." He choked. "Ah! it's strong. I need a little water." He went to the sink and drew water and poured it down so quickly that the water ran from the corners of his mouth and dampened his blue shirt.

Victor was close to the table, passing the glasses. Victor's eyes burned with the quick impact of the whisky. A boldness was growing on him. He waited until Joe Saul came back to the table and then he raised his glass and looked at Mordeen.

"To the Father," he said.

Suddenly Joe Saul's eyes were wet. He drank his drink and slowly put down his glass. He went to Victor and put his arm around the broad young shoulders. "Thank you," he said. "Oh, thank you, Victor."

And Victor in triumph looked again at Mordeen. And he saw hatred in her face as he had never experienced— hatred so cold and dangerous that he could not counter it. His eyes wavered and fell and he turned away, and his eyes met Friend Ed's eyes, and there he saw an executioner looking at him with lethal, detached sternness, as though judging where to put the rope. He coughed and said loudly : "A few more toasts like that and I'd be drunk. I guess I'd better get to work." He went out of the kitchen and his footsteps hammered on the porch boards.

Joe Saul poured more whisky into the glasses. "I'm as skittish as a horse," he said, and he chuckled. "Strange, one moment I want to shout and I find myself weeping. I'm touchy as a range horse in the blowing papers of a picnic ground."

Mordeen stood up carefully. "If we're to have a party, I'd better rest," she said. "The excitement has tired me, tired me out."

"You should eat," Joe Saul said.

"No, not now. Later I'll drink some milk and eat a little toast."

"Lie down then. And if a party is too much, we'll have no party."

"Oh, I want a party—all the friends, the twins, the neighbours. But who's to cook and make the punch?"

"You go," Joe Saul said. "I'll get everything in town. I'll have it sent all ready. It would be a sad thing if I couldn't do this to celebrate our child."

She walked by him and her hand drew lovingly across his back.

Joe Saul watched her go and then he sat down and regarded his poured drink. "I'm tired," he said. "I'm suddenly very tired, as though the blood had poured out of me."

"It's akin to shock," Friend Ed said. "I guess it is a kind of shock. And now if you run true to form, you'll have morning nausea worse than hers, and when there is a little pain in her, your guts will twist in agony. And in labour—oh, God help you, Joe Saul, in labour!"

Joe Saul said : "I want to bring a present to her—some preciousness, some new beautiful thing to delight her, so that her eyes will dance, and she will say : 'Who could ever have thought that I would have a beauty thing like this?'"

"I think she has it."

Joe Saul stirred. "Yes, I know that. But something like a ceremony, something like a golden sacrament, some pearl like a prayer or a red flaring ruby of thanks. Some hard, tangible humility of mine that she can hold in the palm of her hand or wear dangling from a ribbon at her throat. That's a compulsion on me, Friend Ed. Come with me." He was excited again. "I must get this thing. My joy requires a symbol. Come with me to town. We'll get the partiness—all cooked and carved and poured. She's worked so hard before every party that only a little unweariness was left to enjoy it. I'll be the hands to do her work tonight. And then we'll look—I don't know what the beauty is—but I'll know it when I see it."

Now he had made up his mind he was excited again.

"Hurry, Friend Ed. Drink your whisky and come with me. I don't feel trustful of myself to be alone." He walked to the door, and back to the door and back, like a terrier, begging to be let out.

Friend Ed stood up slowly. He said satirically : "Be careful, Joe Saul. Remember the child. See you don't overdo. You must conserve your strength." And then he said seriously : "You don't want to be alone, but do you want Mordeen to be alone ?"

"Ah !" Joe Saul said. "It's hard to remember. She has always been so complete and competent. Thank you for remembering. I'll call Victor, tell him to stay close. I'll take the old dinner-bell to her. Then if she needs anything she can clang the bell and he will come."

Friend Ed said quietly : "I don't think Victor——" and then he knew that he could never say what he had thought.

"Victor's all right. Didn't you hear him ? He's forgot I hit him in the face. Victor's a good boy." He opened the door and shouted "Victor !" and a far answer came. Joe Saul cupped his hands. "Victor, come here, I want to talk to you. Come on, Friend Ed." The two men went out and the door closed behind them. Alone on its shelf the little radio played on, the kettle bustled with steam. The ticking of the clock was very loud.

Now there were steps on the porch. Victor opened the door quietly and stood in the doorway, looking out, while an automobile engine roared and the sound whined up the gears and slowly rose to silence in the distance. Then Victor gently closed the door and walked lightly to the table. He poured himself a drink and drained the glass and quickly poured another. The neck of the bottle clashed against the tumbler. And through the open door to the bedroom Mordeen's voice called : "Is it you, Joe Saul ?"

Victor sat quietly and sipped his drink, and his glance rose and remained on the door. He sat down in one of the straight chairs and leaned back, and the old chair creaked. Mordeen called anxiously : "Who's there ?" And in a moment she stood in the doorway. She saw Victor and stopped and her hands went out and braced against the door frame. "Oh!" she said. "It's you. Why didn't you answer?"

Victor rocked his chair a little on its hind legs and he sipped the straight whisky in his glass. "Joe Saul asked me to take care of you while he's in town. He told me to, ordered me to."

"What do you want, Victor?" she asked in alarm. "You shouldn't be drinking now."

He finished the drink and idly poured another. His eyes felt over her body. "Come in," he said. "Come in and sit and talk to me."

For a moment she hesitated, and then her face became a mask, closed and wary and waiting. She crossed behind the table and sat down on the cot under the window. Outside a cow bawled mournfully for her calf.

Mordeen said woodenly, and softly: "What do you want, Victor?"

He swung his chair round, facing her. He rested his elbow on the table and he crossed his legs. "Just wanted to pass the time of day with you," he said. "I never seem to get to talk to you. Isn't that funny? I'd think you'd want to talk to me."

She stared at him, her eyes expressionless.

Victor tasted his drink and made himself more comfortable. His body slouched in his chair. The small gold medal shone at his throat. "And now I hear this interesting news, but not from you. I hear it from Old Joe Saul. It just seemed to me that you yourself would want to tell me all about it."

She said finally in a monotone: "When you finish your game, maybe you'll tell me what you want."

Victor smiled. "You don't want to pretend that you don't know what I'm talking about, do you?"

"I know what you're talking about," she said, "but I don't know what you are trying to say."

He uncrossed his legs and leaned towards her. "Do you think I have no interest in my child?" he asked.

She said without emphasis : "It's not your child, Victor. It's Joe Saul's child."

Now he laughed loudly. "Mordeen," he said, "do you think that if you say that often enough it will be true?"

"It is true," she said.

Now he leaped up angrily. "That's a lie," he cried. "You know it is and I know it is. You know Joe Saul can't have a child. You know that. I don't like being used. I don't like being shut out of something that's mine. Don't try tricks, because I don't like them. This is my baby. I've got a lot of girls in trouble, so I know *I'm* all right—but this is the first one that will be born. Don't you think I have some feeling for my own blood? Do you think I want to be used like a stud animal for the comfort of Joe Saul? Is that fair? He gets everything, and I get put back in the corral."

"You got what you said you wanted," she said coldly. "You got what you can understand."

"Don't do that again," he said angrily. "What I can understand and what I can't understand! I think I proved to you I could understand anything you can. Even if you wouldn't come near me again afterwards."

She said : "Victor, don't bother me."

"Don't bother you. First I don't understand and now don't bother you. I understand enough to be sure it's my child, and I'll bother you when you have my baby. Understand that!" He leaned towards her in rage, beating out his intention on the table with his closed fist.

His anger raised anger in her. She stood up and her voice fought against the control she put on it. "I told you, Victor, and asked and even begged you to believe that I would do anything in the world for Joe Saul's content because of my love for him."

"Yah!" he said snarlingly.

"I tell you again. I warn you to believe it."

"What's he going to say when he knows it's my baby,

when he knows you were out in the barn with me when he was drunk?"

She cried fiercely: "It's Joe Saul's baby, conceived in love for him. I saw his face hovering over me. I felt his arms—not yours. You don't exist in this, Victor. The little seed may have been yours, I have forgotten. But no love was given or offered or taken. No! It's Joe Saul's baby. Joe Saul's and mine."

She glared at him like a mother cat, and her claws were out. And then she backed to the cot, her teeth bared and her nostrils flaring. She breathed in little bursts. "And no one, nothing will take that away. I had to do an alien thing, had to hide my hurt in a mountain cave of love to do it. You nor any consideration will take this child away from Joe Saul. Believe it, Victor. If I could do that thing before—think what I could do now."

Victor's body and face were beaten by her force. He stood, walked towards the door. And suddenly he flung himself on the floor in front of her and embraced her ankles and laid his face down on her feet.

"Oh, God! I'm lonely." His despair was heavy as a grey stone. "What have I done, Mordeen? What crime have I committed? In the night I've thought of the things you said. Mordeen, I've laughed at them and I've run out to women to prove those words weren't true—and they are." He raised his face and looked at her. "I wish I had never seen Joe Saul. I wish I had never seen your eyes on him hot and happy and shining. If I had not known, I could go to the town girls, fumble at their dresses, quiet their giggling and rut them. But now I hear your voice over their little shrill squeals of pleased protest. I feel your strong sure warmth behind their chilly pimpled breasts." He said miserably: "I love you. And it's not like anything I have ever known. It is as different as—as—you said it once—as milk."

Her face had grown compassionate as she looked down at him. "Poor Victor, you will find it. If you are open to it, capable of returning it, this will come to you."

"I've argued this way, argued to myself, Mordeen. But I have found this kind of love, and it cries in my mind that it can't happen twice." He rose up to his knees. "It shouts to me that if I do not save this—this one I know beyond all doubt—I will lose my chance. Mordeen," he cried, "I'm frantic. I do not think I can live. I don't say this the way such things are said—I do not think I can live. I have a crazy animal clawing in my guts." And indeed he was doubled up with pain.

"Now you know," she said softly. "Now you know why I did what I did. I didn't think you were capable of knowing." In pity she put her hand on his forehead and smoothed his hair back. Outside, a thunderhead throttled the sun and the light in the kitchen grew dusky. The radio turned low intoned prices of wheat, barley, corn, oats, hay, hogs, steers, calves, sheep, in a murmured litany.

Mordeen said : "I guess a shower is coming. Can't you go away, Victor? If you feel so, wouldn't it be better if you were not here, because this pattern will not change? Nothing can change it. You've thought of killing Joe Saul, haven't you, Victor?"

"Yes," he said almost under his breath.

"That would not change it. I would still be Joe Saul's wife, and this one here would be his child. And you, Victor, would be colder than a lonely cold; you would die in the cold of hatred. Think carefully of going away. The year will turn, and it will be better and then better and then—gone in some best new thing."

The kitchen was quite dark now and a very far thunder rumble shook the air. Victor put his cheek down on her knees, and time and the year rolled over and over as the earth rolls, swaying like a tiring top. The year changed and the world swung through the great ellipse. The year and the season swung on about the house. In Mordeen the baby grew. And the year rolled on.

"I've thought of that too," Victor said. "I can say with my mind that I will go—but I would refuse it. That I know. For I think of the summer ending now and the stubble on the ground and the hay brushing the ridge-pole in the barn and windfall apples on the orchard earth. And you—a swelling below your breasts and my child kicking against the soft wall, and turning, and I not able to put my hand there and feel its moving life."

"Hush, Victor. It is not your child. A year will draw— is drawing—out your sorrow like a basting thread."

"A year," he said in the darkened room. And thunder crashed distantly and a blue flickering flash shook the room. "I know the passing year. The autumn is chilling down and the hoar frost does crisp and yellow the strong grasses near the stream under the tattering cottonwoods. The blackbirds flocked nervously a week and now they are gone. The wind and the arrowing wild ducks are driving to the south over the burning sumac. And you—you walk heavily on your heels, your shoulders back to balance the growing weight of my child, and your face is glorious and your eyes smile all day long and your mouth perhaps turns upward, smiling in your sleep."

"Hush, Victor," she said wearily. "It's not your child. And don't you think it is a little cold in here? The rain will turn to sleet, I think."

The year slipped past, and the endless business of the ageing earth continued.

The wind whined a little ghost howl around the corners of the house.

"A man can forget nearly anything in a year, Victor."

"I know this year," he said miserably. "I know the white drifts curving down to the silver ice in the shallows above the pond. I know the black lashing branches of the pear trees and the dogs snuffling and moaning in the storm porch. I can feel the ice-air burning in my nose and blue aching finger-nails and the acid cider. They're bringing in a Christmas tree from the forest today. And you, Mordeen, quiet and tired with waiting—you move silently, with eyes and ears and touch turned inward to hear and see and feel my child."

She stirred in the steely light, moved heavily. "It's not your child. It's Joe Saul's child," she said with heavy monotony. "Turn on the light, Victor, and build up the fire. The cold is creeping in. The winter's really here. My year of bearing is nearly done. And very soon Friend Ed and Joe Saul will be coming with the Christmas tree. Shovel a wider path down to the road so they can get the tree in. They said it would touch the ceiling. And, Victor, I wish you could find the strength to go away. I've seen your suffering in this livelong year. But the birth will be soon now, Victor. Please try to go away. I have not changed my mind in the year. It's Joe Saul's child. I will protect him in this child. I threaten you, Victor."

He cried : "Mordeen, I love you. I cannot go away."

He stood up and turned on the light, opened the stove and poked the dying fire to flame. The light was nearly gone. The windows were edged with white and big feathered flakes were drifting down.

The steel winter lay on the land and crept to the doors and windows and peered whitely in. And the snow put silence on the earth. Mordeen pushed herself heavily up from the couch. Her shoulders were back and the child was low and large in her body. She shuffled across the room, filled the tea-kettle, and put it on the stove. One of her hands stayed on her abdomen, as though to help support the weight which bore her down. Then she stood listening. "I think they're coming in. Go help them, Victor; help them get it through the door. And please remember what I said."

Victor looked out, and then he opened the porch door. A tumble of snow came in. Friend Ed and Joe Saul were sliding the fine fir-tree butt forward up the path. They edged it up the stairs to the open door and Victor grabbed it and pulled the snowy branches through the door. Joe Saul and Friend Ed stood on the storm porch, stamping and beating their shoulders. They stood laughing there, taking off their coats and kicking the arctics from their feet, and then they came into the pleasant kitchen. Their cheeks were pink with cold and their eyes watered. They rubbed their hands together in the warmth.

"We'll have to cut it off," Friend Ed observed. "I told you it was too big."

Mordeen had brought a broom to sweep up the scattered snow before it melted. She moved slowly with a careful rolling step.

Joe Saul cried: "I'd rather have it too big and cut it off than too small and have to stretch it. Here, give me that broom, Mordeen. You shouldn't be doing that. Here, you sit down and let us do all this."

She smiled, saying: "It's been hard learning not to do my own work. You may regret you've made a sluggard of your wife."

"You'll learn to do it again." Joe Saul laughed. "But not now. The work you are doing is much more important. I was telling Friend Ed how startled I was when the baby moved—lying in bed, and I guess I was half asleep, and when I felt this little secret movement, and it awakened me." He looked upward, smiling in his remembering. "At first it was as though someone had touched me to catch my attention, but very gently. And then I felt a creeping like a soft cat—stealthy. And then there was a little push, and then—you can believe this or not—there was a shaking like silent laughter and then a scrabbling movement. I felt it climb up my spine and then come tumbling down again. And then the small shake of laughing. Well, it startled me. I thought at first one of the dogs had crawled in bed with us. And I sat up and turned on the light. Mordeen didn't even wake up. And do you know what it was?" He pointed. "It was that one playing in the darkness of his mother." He laughed with pleasure, and Mordeen smiled. Victor moved restlessly.

Friend Ed said: "I know how that is. And if you want to feel a real rumpus, you have twins some time. I think they play volley ball. The doctor didn't say it's twins, did he, Mordeen?"

"No," she said, "it's only one. And it's turned and perfect. I saw it," she said in wonder. "I saw it on the X-ray plate. At first I didn't know what it was. Know what it looked like? Well, it looked like the nave of a cathedral with a vaulted roof and one great column—that was ribs and spine. At first I couldn't make out the child until Dr Zorn showed me, and then, there he was, upside down and balled up like a kitten."

Joe Saul said excitedly: "What did he look like, what could you see?"

"Why, everything," she said. "His head and little arms and his legs and feet curled up. He's been a great jumper, but now he's quiet. That worried me. I thought something might be wrong. But Dr Zorn says he's just fine. He will be quiet now, the doctor says. He will sleep until he has to make the big fight."

Victor said nervously: "If you aren't going to set up the tree right now, I'd like to go out to my room. I don't feel clean."

"Go ahead," Joe Saul agreed. "We'll put up the tree after dinner." And Victor said: "I don't feel clean," and he almost ran from the room. Mordeen watched him go.

"I don't know how we'll get around that monster tree," Mordeen said. "It will nearly fill the room."

"And ought to," Joe Saul crowed. "Say, I'd like to see that picture. I wonder if I could get it."

"The doctor wants to study it," Mordeen said. "But if you go to his office I'm sure he'll show it to you."

"Maybe afterwards he'll let me have it to keep," said Joe Saul. He sat down by the table and stretched his arms in luxury. "Next Christmas, Friend Ed, next tree we bring in—why, he'll be sitting under it. And he'll have his own presents. I wonder what I'll get him his first Christmas. I'll have to think about that. But I've got a whole year to think."

"Something round or soft or shiny the first year," Friend Ed advised. "That's about all that interests them the first year. Say, you'd better not call 'him' all the time. It might be a girl."

"I don't care," Joe Saul said. "I'd like a girl. I'll like what I get." He turned to Mordeen. "You go in the bedroom and lie down and rest," he ordered. "I'm going to get dinner now. I'll call you when it's ready. Friend Ed is going to eat with us. He'll help me."

She stood up slowly and obediently. "I'm really spoiled," she said, smiling. "And I like it very well. You have a lazy wife, and it is your fault."

He stood up and went to her and took her face between his hands and looked in her eyes, holding her chin tilted up at him. And he chuckled with delight. "Look, only look, Friend Ed. Isn't she beautiful?" And suddenly his lips trembled and he looked away. And Mordeen moved heavily through the door.

Joe Saul stirred the fire and put a big pan on the heat. "It's going to be a fry supper," he said. "Whether you like it or not, that's what you'll get, Friend Ed." He moved quickly about at his preparation. "Fried liver and stewed tomatoes and milk and tapioca for dessert. Would you like a drink of whisky, Friend Ed?"

"I wouldn't mind."

Joe Saul brought bottle and glasses to the table and poured two big drinks. "It will take a minute for the pan to heat," he said. "Everything's ready. I did it all this morning. When I fry the liver we can eat." He drank half of his whisky and set the glass down on the table. "It's strange, Friend Ed," he said. "Of course you know the baby's there—of course it's there—but it's a mystery. I suppose you don't quite believe it until it is really born. But she has *seen* it, really seen the head and arms and legs. That's different! That's a very different thing. That makes it real. It's not just an idea any more or a wish or a prayer. It's a real thing. Oh, I'll have to see that picture! I'll have to see it. I'll go tomorrow."

"I see what you mean, Joe Saul. That's true."

The door burst open and Victor stood before them. His eyes were wild. He was wrapped in an overcoat and he carried a suitcase in his hand.

"I can't stand it. I'm getting out. I'm going—going now—right now!"

Joe Saul looked at him in amazement. "Going? What's wrong with you, Victor?"

"Well, I—I can't stand it, that's all."

"Can't you tell me what's the matter?" Joe Saul asked.

A torturing struggle was taking place in Victor's mind. His eyes were filled with fierce suffering, with hatred and longing and love.

Joe Saul asked: "Is it because I hit you in the face, Victor?"

For a moment Victor was still weighing, fighting with himself, and at last he chose his course. He looked at Joe Saul almost with compassion. "That's it," he said. "I can't stay in a place where I was hit in the face."

"But I apologized," said Joe Saul. "I said I was sorry. Did it hurt so much, Victor?"

"Yes, it did."

"I'm sorry. In a time of such joy, it seems a shame. Isn't there anything I can do?"

Victor fought himself, and his emotion overcame him. "No," he cried. "No. I'm going." He turned and ran as though he could not trust himself. He ran out of the door and left it standing open.

Joe Saul sighed. He went to the door and looked out and then he closed it gently and came back to the table. "I thought he had forgotten," he said. "I'm sorry he feels this way. He didn't even tell me where to send his pay."

Friend Ed spoke uneasily. "Let him go. He's young, and that's a brooding time, Joe Saul. That's a time when you inspect your hurts like little rocks. Let him go. There are many Victors. There will always be a Victor."

"I suppose you are right. I wish I had not hit him. I'm ashamed of that."

"Maybe he is ashamed too."

"Of what?"

"Of—running away."

"I'm sad because I was weak. I would not like to give weakness to my child."

He drank the rest of his whisky. "Remember, I said next year he'll have a present of his own. But he's a real thing now, with the picture. He's there and I can see him. He's closer than in another room. There's just a little soft wall between. Maybe he can hear and feel. I'm giving him a present soon."

"You're crazy, Joe Saul. You're just dog-crazy."

"Maybe I am, but that's how I hope to stay. I had a strange thought. He's there, he's here. Why shouldn't he have a present this year? Why should he not?"

Friend Ed grinned. "Might be a little difficult to give to him. You're crazy, Joe Saul."

"Well, I could give him a present. I thought what I could give him. If I had the weakness to hit Victor, maybe I have others. I thought of it when I wanted to go in to Dr Zorn to see the picture, and now I think of it more. I want to give my son clean blood."

"You have," Friend Ed said uneasily. "What are you talking about?"

"I want to give him the proof. That's what I mean—attested. I can get Zorn to go over me, head, heart, stomach, everything. Maybe I can say to this child—that's what your father gave you first of all—strength and health and cleanliness. That would not be a bad present, Friend Ed."

"I think you're really crazy," he said anxiously. "This is a silly thing. I don't like it. I don't want you to do it."

"*You* don't. Why don't you? I can give the papers all signed by Dr Zorn—maybe rolled like a parchment with a big seal and tied with a red ribbon like a diploma. I could hang it on the tree for him. His first present and the best."

"Don't do it. Zorn might think you're crazy, the way I do. He might put that in your paper."

But Joe Saul poured whisky in both glasses. He leaned across the table towards Friend Ed. "Don't tell Mordeen.

138

I'll do it as a secret and as a kind of joke, but not a joke too. I haven't ever had a thorough check-up. It will please her, Friend Ed; don't tell her."

Friend Ed stood up. "I don't want you to do this. I don't like this. It's—it's crazy."

Joe Saul said quietly: "I think it is the sanest thing I have ever done. I don't know why I haven't done it before."

He raised his glass and cried: "I'm giving him a present. I must be sure it is perfect. I'm giving him the greatest present in the world. I'm giving my son *life*."

ACT THREE, SCENE I

THE SEA

THE tiny cabin of the little freighter was old and comfortable and well used. On one side stood a little mess-table with a retaining ridge; good swivel-chairs were bolted to the floor, and water-bottles and glasses were placed in racks on a small sideboard. The walls were panelled in dark wood well oiled and rubbed for many years, and the bright brass-work shone. Against one wall, under hanging sea coats, was a broad chest upholstered as a bench. Two deep leather chairs stood in front of a small coal grate in a tile mantel, and on the mantel itself there was a model of a schooner complete and beautiful in its detail; beside it was a small artificial Christmas tree decorated with tinsel and silver and red glass balls. On the little hearth was a small rack of fire tools—a short heavy poker, a shovel, and tongs. On the wall under the port-holes hung the trophies of many voyages to many places, assegai and knobkerries from Africa, war clubs and shark-toothed spears from the Polynesian south, daggers and stilettos, a witch mask or two, and a shrunken head, black and baleful, hanging by its hair.

The door stood open to the rail of the flying bridge and beyond—the night city of docks and behind them tall lighted buildings, and neon signs glowing in the sky. A second closed door led to the sleeping-cabins. A small coal fire glowed in the iron grate.

From outside came the sounds of the harbour, toot of tugs and mutter of engines, and steam hiss and rumble of deck winches and creak of lines in running gear. Behind the harbour sounds the city talked with street-cars and truck engines, with motor horns and juke-box music.

Mr Victor in a blue mate's uniform and cap came into the cabin. He looked around nervously, then went to the little grate and stirred the coals, rattled the poker on the iron. A tug whistled a passing signal in the stream. And in the city a fire siren whined up the scale and down again. Mr Victor stood looking at the little Christmas tree on the mantel. From the other side of the closed door Mordeen's voice came, muffled, calling: "Joe Saul!" Mr Victor's head swung round. "Joe Saul!" the voice called with a note of alarm in it.

Mr Victor went to the door and opened it. "He's not here," he said. "Come out, I want to talk to you." He went back to the grate and rubbed his hands close to the coals, and he said again towards the open door: "Come here, Mordeen. I want to talk to you."

In a moment she stood in the doorway, her hair dishevelled from the pillow and her eyes wild and uncertain with sleep. She said: "I had a dream." And then as her mind came out of sleep: "Where did Joe Saul go?"

"He went ashore," said Mr Victor. "He told me to stand by in case you needed anything."

"The time is close, Victor," she said. "I've had the first ragged pains. Maybe false pains, but my time is close. I want Joe Saul here with me. I want him here." She walked back and forth in the heavy, rolling pace that restlessly precedes birth.

"Sit down," said Mr Victor.

"No," she said. "I'm not comfortable sitting down." And then she laughed shortly. "A woman told me she always could tell when a child was due because she cleaned the bottom drawers of her bureau. Well, I just remembered the dust in the bottom of my cabinet, and I wanted to bend down, way down, to clean it out. I guess that's my sign. I want Joe Saul here. If he does not come back soon, I want you to look for him, Victor. It will be soon —oh, very soon."

A seething excitement filled Victor. He moved one of the big chairs a little. "No," he said at last, quietly but with a force controlled in his throat. "I can't! I tried, Mordeen. I tried to force myself. And I know that if it goes on a little more I will not—I will not know what I am doing." He held out his arms and he cried : "See, a chill is going on in me. My hands won't be quiet. Mordeen, I can't let you go."

"Let me go, Victor? What are you saying?" Her face was alarmed.

"I've given it every thought," he cried. "I can't do it. You are my woman and that is my child. I must have you."

"Are you crazy?" She stood in front of him. "I am not your woman!"

"Maybe crazy," he said. "And maybe I will get crazier. You must come away with me now. You are my woman and I cannot have my child born here."

"Mr Victor," she said in command. "Go to your quarters. Go instantly. If Joe Saul heard you, he would have you off the ship or he would kill you. Go to your quarters!"

"No," he said, wondering. "It's too late. I must have you and my child." The hysterical intensity grew in his voice. "I must have that. It would be good if you wanted me as much as I want you, but I must have you whether you wish it or not. This is my whole life. I won't throw it away no matter what comes of it. Look!" he cried. "I tried to run away and leave you and my child to Old Joe Saul. And I couldn't do it. I came back. And I tried to be wise—to stand by like a cuckolded goat and see my woman and my child in Joe Saul's arms. *And I cannot do it*."

"Victor," she said, "I've told you over and over why I need this child : I love Joe Saul. This is crazy."

"Crazy or not, that's the way it is," he said dully. "I will not lose the one life I have ever had—even if the world burns up."

She said kindly : "Poor Victor. You do not understand many things, and this you don't seem to understand at all."

"Maybe I don't have to understand," he said. "You are going away with me—now, tonight. I have a place for you. I have a doctor. You will come with me now. You must come with me now"—his voice rose—"if I have to tear you free."

She was frightened at him now, sensing his growing hysteria. "I will not go, Victor. Don't you know that? Nothing can make me go. Don't you know that?"

His head was down and he shook it slowly from side to side. "There's only one other thing," he said. "We can wait here—just as we are. When Joe Saul comes I will tell him. I will tell him everything. I don't think you can look into his eyes and say : 'This is not true.' Then he will throw you out, and I will take you. In his rage he may hurt you—and the child. Is this worth doing, Mordeen? Or suppose he didn't—suppose he let it pass and you had to live with his covered hatred for you and his hatred for my child. I will surely tell him, Mordeen. Even if I don't want to I will surely do it."

Her body bent over with pain. She leaned forward and her eyes distended and she bit her lips until the pain receded.

"It's starting. Give me time," she begged. "Please, Victor, give me time to think. I can't think now. Can't you see?"

"No," he said. "I've been over it too often in my mind. I don't dare give you time. No. I can't afford to give you time. It would cheat me," he shouted. "I tell you I don't dare. You must come away."

"I won't go," she said. "He will understand, and it will be all right."

"You don't believe that, Mordeen. If that were so, why didn't he adopt a child? Why his constant talk about blood and family? No, you don't believe that."

She came to him, pleading then. "Please, Victor, don't destroy three people for the sake of one. He has never hurt you. Why will you kill him, and through him me? What will you have then? Please, Victor. At least give me a little time."

"No," he said. "Time? Time is my enemy."

Suddenly she was calm and very tired. "Victor, many things have happened. With the child forming and growing in my womb, there is also a change in my mind. I am not the same as before. The hard self-corners are smoothed."

He asked uneasily: "Is this some trick?"

"No," she said quietly. "I don't think it is a trick, unless it is a trick on me too. At first when I asked your help I was closed off in a little house of pain. There were no others in my world except Joe Saul and me. But in the long heavy months my world has grown. It is not closed off."

Victor said restlessly: "What are you trying to do?"

"I'm trying to tell you that you could be welcome now."

"How about Joe Saul?" he demanded.

"That has not changed. I love Joe Saul. I will not have him hurt. I am his wife."

"What kind of fool do you think I am? Are you saying you would love both of us?" he demanded.

"Not in the way you mean, Victor. But I would try to open the family like a garment and take you in."

"Do you think you could be wife to two men?"

143

"No, Victor. I can be wife only to Joe Saul."

"Then I say no," he cried. "No!"

She looked at him closely then to make sure he would not change. "Please, Victor."

"No."

"Victor," she cried, "you don't know what your choice means! You don't know me. Please, Victor. You don't know. Why should you throw your life away? Don't do it, Victor! I beg you not to do it."

He said dully: "I've thought about it long, Mordeen. Lying in my bunk, hearing you laughing and planning with Joe Saul—how do you think that feels? Mordeen, if my choice were made with the certainty that I would die tomorrow, I would still make it. You must come away."

"You're sure, Victor? Can't there be some change? Can't you give me—at least a little time? Please, Victor—time."

"No," he said. "I can't go back now. I'm in a long narrow tunnel and I can't turn."

For a long moment she looked at him, and her eyes were full of tears. Neither of them saw Friend Ed standing at the doorway, looking in at them. His dark blue captain's uniform concealed his figure in the half-darkness.

Mordeen shook her head slowly. "I don't have a choice?" she said.

"No, you don't have a choice. Get a coat. That's all you have to take. Everything will be new—everything."

She sighed deeply. "Don't you know I will kill you, Victor?"

"Hurry," he said. "Only a coat. I don't want anything more from this old life."

She looked at him quietly, and her eyes set with resolve. She moved to the rack of coats and lifted down a long grey cloak.

"Victor," she said, "will you get the suitcase under my bunk?"

"What suitcase?" he demanded suspiciously. "I don't want anything from this life."

She turned towards him. "It's for the hospital," she said. "I've had it packed for weeks."

He hesitated.

"Get it, Victor," she said.

He went to the door, and as he passed through she hurried to the relics on the wall and drew a short thick knife from its sheath and concealed it in the folds of her cloak. And as she did, she saw Friend Ed standing just inside the door, shaking his head slowly at her. She stood perfectly still, her mouth open a little.

Victor came from the sleeping-cabin carrying the suitcase. He saw Friend Ed. He dropped the suitcase on the floor and moved quickly towards him.

"What the hell do you want?" he demanded.

But Friend Ed looked past him at Mordeen. "Once I wouldn't help you," he said. "I wouldn't take the responsibility. Now I will."

"Get out of here!" Victor said.

"Hush," said Friend Ed.

Mordeen said: "I did it all myself. I don't need your help."

"But you have it now," Friend Ed said. "Whether you want it or not, you have it."

"Stay clear!" she shouted at him. "Stay clear of this! What I have started I will finish."

"I have my sailing orders," he said. "I sail at midnight. I came to say goodbye." He looked at Victor. "Will you come on deck with me?" he asked. "I have a message for you."

"Say it here," Victor said harshly.

"No, it's a secret. Come!" He gently urged Victor through the door, and the two disappeared into the night.

Mordeen stood rigid, her eyes wide with fright. She waited for what she expected—then came the crunching blow, the expelled moaning cry, and in a moment the little splash. She shivered.

She was still staring straight ahead when Friend Ed came in again. He walked over to her and gently took the knife from her and replaced it in its sheath. He came back to her and took her arm and helped her to a chair and seated her.

He said : "Where's Joe Saul? I came to say goodbye."

She roused herself from shock. "He was not bad, Friend Ed. He was not evil."

"I know," he said.

"I can't think," she said. "It's coming—the pains are coming."

Joe Saul stood in the open door, his legs apart, his shoulders down; his chin was hard with rage and his eyes flared with fury. Mordeen moved towards him. Then she saw his hard eyes that looked through and past her, and she moved timidly to the chest under the hanging coats, as though to hide.

Friend Ed cried : "I've been looking for you. I've got my orders. I'm sailing at midnight. What's the matter with you, Joe Saul? Have you been drinking?"

"Drinking? No," he cried in rage. "I'm a sick man. That's what. I'm—sick!"

Friend Ed spoke in despair. "You went to Dr Zorn!"

"Yes, I went. I went. I went all by myself. No one asked me to go. Goddamit, no one asked me to go!"

Friend Ed said hopelessly : "You went to Dr Zorn. You know!"

Mordeen embraced herself in silent agony.

Joe Saul's eyes became wary. He did not meet Friend Ed's eyes. He did not look at Mordeen. "It's my heart. Doc Zorn says I have a bad heart. Me—a bad heart. I was sick once when I was a boy. That caused it."

Friend Ed spoke to Joe Saul as though he were a child. "Well, is it dangerous?"

Joe Saul cried : "Dangerous! He says I'll have to take it easy. Take it easy—me!"

Friend Ed sat in a swivel-chair at the end of the table and laughed and laughed. "What's wrong with that?

Might be a good thing to take it easy. I'd like to myself. Give you more time with the baby."

Joe Saul said venomously : "I guess so. Mr Victor has read all the books—now he can do some work."

Mordeen covered her face with her hands.

Friend Ed said : "Forget Victor. Victor is not here."

But Joe Saul went on, unhearing. "Some day he'll be master of a big liner, ladies and the captain's dinner, and he'll go up to the bridge once every watch just to see that everything's all right—but the sea's not in him. It will be a big hotel floating back and forth—maybe so big that they don't even turn it round—like a ferry-boat."

"Stop it," Friend Ed said. "Don't blame Victor."

And Joe Saul said harshly : "At the bleak opening of the world we edged along the points in burned-out logs, feeling the coasts. We were sailors. Then with rush sails on cross-tied sticks we moved over the waters, and we raised a little light on the world so that it was not edged in darkness. We shipped long sweeps to beat against the winds and currents. We ranged up the coasts, up and down, from Sidon to Cornwall, from Carthage to Good Hope. And then—oh, timidly we put out into the blackness, crept blindly out and found it was not black at all but another bright world. We knew by roll and creak, by smell and the patterned flight of birds, by brown mud in the sea or floating weeds or a tormented school of herring how it was with the world and with the weather."

Friend Ed said quickly : "Be sure you aren't lying, Joe Saul."

But Joe Saul went on bitterly : "Mr Victor's all right, and if he's not sure he has a book. But he does not see without looking nor hear without listening. When we came in the harbour he nearly ran down a scow because his hand did not swing over. He had to think and we nearly cut the scow in two. But I was there. Maybe now I will not be there. Maybe another time I'll be in my bunk, a sick man, and on the bridge—Mr Victor. And I'm the one who wanted to give a present—a present of perfection —a Christmas present."

Friend Ed stood up and walked to the grate and warmed his hands for a moment while he thought. He moved the glowing coals with the short poker. And suddenly he made his decision. He touched Mordeen on the shoulder and strode back to stand over Joe Saul. "You're lying to me, Joe Saul. I don't remember any time before when you had to lie to me. And I would let you lie and gradually come out with your nasty truth, but there's no time. I'm sailing at midnight. So drop your lie."

Joe Saul asked : "What lie?"

"You know what lie. Your heart. That's not it, Joe Saul, and you know it. After all this time you've dug up your hard icy fact and finally you've got to face it. And if I'm to help you as my right and duty say, then I've got to help you with the truth. Name it, Joe Saul, name it, goddam you !"

Joe Saul shivered and his body shrank and he sat down heavily in one of the swivel-chairs. His mouth worked helplessly. He said : "I forced it. Zorn didn't want me to see. I forced him. I made him let me see. I was crazy with power and joyfulness. I told him I would go to another man if he did not let me see. I made him let me look in the microscope."

Mordeen stood up and gripped the mantel with her hands. Friend Ed glanced at her and then moved a little to cover the sight of her from Joe Saul. Friend Ed said : "For a fool a happy lie is good enough. But I had hoped you were a little wiser. If you were wiser, the truth could be a glory for you."

Joe Saul went on : "I made him let me look. I saw the slide—big as a port-hole it looked, and blinding with light. I turned the knob, and there they were, I saw them —shrunken and crooked and dead, corpses of sperm— dead. And, oh, my God !" Joe Saul covered his eyes with his hands.

Friend Ed got up and stood over his friend in pity. He

148

tried to think. "I haven't much time," he said. "What can I do for you, Joe Saul?"

Joe Saul spoke behind his hands. "What can anyone do? It is finished. My line, my blood, all the procession of the ages is dead. And I am only waiting a little while and then I die."

Friend Ed sighed. He looked to Mordeen for help and then he chose his hard course.

"What are you going to do, Joe Saul?" he said harshly. "Take down your hands. Stop trying to hide in the dark behind your fingers. The world still goes on outside. What are you going to do? What are you going to think? I haven't got much time."

Joe Saul raised his head. "I haven't had much time to think," he said.

"You've had all your life to think. You haven't dared."

Now rage came flooding up in Joe Saul's body and in his mind. "I'll have to kill him," he said hoarsely. "There is no place in the whole world for him to live, knowing and sneering, maybe never telling but always knowing. I cannot have his mind living in the same world with me."

Friend Ed said : "Forget Victor, forget Victor. How about Mordeen?"

Joe Saul bared his teeth and looked at the wall in front of him. "I can't get my mind open to her treachery. I feel that if I let myself look at her or think even for a second about her that I'll go down in a horrible pit with my hands on her throat. Stop torturing me, Friend Ed! Stop torturing me!" And Joe Saul covered his eyes again and his body shook. "There's no place for me to live in the whole world," he said.

Mordeen crept to the chair and hid in it.

Friend Ed's voice cut into Joe Saul like a wet rawhide thong. "Stand up, you cowardly, dirty thing! Stand up, or by Christ I'll hit you sitting down! Stand up!"

Joe Saul looked up in wonder at this rage. He came slowly to his feet. "What's this, Friend Ed?"

"Friend nothing. So much I can take and no more.

What is this crawling, whining ego of yours that's so important? How can you dare out of your silly self to crush a lovely thing? Have I wasted my life being friend to a whimpering nastiness?"

"Friend Ed, what are you saying? Don't you understand?"

"I do understand. I understand that you are offered a loveliness and you vomit on it, that you have the gift of love given you such as few men have ever known and you throw on it the acid of your pride, your ugly twisted sense of importance."

"Friend Ed, Friend Ed, don't you understand? It's not my child, it can't be."

"It *is* your child. More than you can conceive in your sick soul. Soul? I wonder what your soul looks like. I think I know—it looks like those dead shrunken sperm." Friend Ed's voice spat at him so that Joe Saul raised his hands as though to protect himself from blows.

"She is giving you a child—yours—to be your own. Her love for you is so great that she could do a thing that was strange and foul to her and yet not be dirtied by it. She ringed herself with love and beauty to give you love and beauty. How wrong she must have been to love a fool—and a filthy fool."

"But why couldn't she tell me? Why did I have to discover——"

"Because you couldn't receive it. Because in your smallness you had not the graciousness to receive this gift. You cannot live because you have not ever looked at life. You crush loveliness on the rocks of your stinking pride. I wonder if you ever could understand." Friend Ed stood towering over Joe Saul and suddenly, without warning, struck him in the face with his open hand, struck him with complete contempt.

Joe Saul's eyes were wide. His hand rose slowly and touched his reddening cheek. And he looked at his fingers. His body sank slowly into the chair, but his eyes, wide with wonder and confusion and pain, did not leave Friend Ed's face.

And Friend Ed's mouth trembled and his eyes were sad. He kneeled down beside the chair and put his arm round Joe Saul's shoulders. "I've given you everything a friend can give, Joe Saul—even contempt, and that's the hardest thing of all. Killing is easy compared to that." And he said : "You didn't hear what I had to say. I'm sailing at midnight. I've done everything I can—everything. Now you will be all alone on your particular dark ocean. Maybe your soul will require the destruction of everything beautiful around it for its small integrity. But I always thought it might be a little braver soul than that, Joe Saul. It is so easy a thing to give—only great men have the courage and courtesy and, yes, the generosity to receive."

Joe Saul looked blankly away from Friend Ed and closed his eyes.

Friend Ed went on : "Now you are alone. I don't know what you will do or think. But I can't believe, I can't think, that all my life I have been a friend to meanness."

Joe Saul's eyes wandered away and then came back. "Don't leave me, Friend Ed ! For God's sake, don't leave me alone ! I'm afraid. I don't know what to do." His voice was pleading. "Don't leave me alone !"

Friend Ed spoke softly. "I told you—I have my sailing orders. I have to go."

"I'm afraid. I don't know what to do."

"I don't know what you'll do, Joe Saul. But I would hope that some greatness might be left in you. They say that crippled men have compensations which make them stronger than the strong. I could wish that you would know and understand that you are the husband and the father of love. The gift you have received is beyond the furthest hope of most men. It's not that you should try to excuse or explain. You should—you must—search in your dark crippled self for the goodness and the generosity to receive."

Joe Saul looked at him in wonder. "Are you sure that this is true, Friend Ed?"

"I am sure—oh, I am sure. But you—if you ever require sureness you have a long twilight way to go."

Joe Saul said: "It's a new, an unknown road. I don't know that I can find it alone."

"You'll never find it any other way. Come, say good-bye to me, Joe Saul. Say a good wish to me standing off to sea, and to yourself—standing off. Come, Joe Saul. Take the first steps. Come, Joe Saul." His hand put a little pressure behind Joe Saul's shoulders and almost forced him to his feet. Friend Ed took Joe Saul's cap from the table and put it on his head and straightened it. And he buttoned the two top gold buttons of Joe Saul's uniform.

Joe Saul said brokenly: "Friend Ed——"

"Hush. You'll have to work it out. You'll have to work it out—alone."

He pushed Joe Saul out and stood with him against the rail. And then Friend Ed came back and stood in the doorway looking into Mordeen's eyes. And he bowed with respect and love. Then he went quickly away. Joe Saul stood gazing after him.

Mordeen got up and moved towards the door, and then a great convulsion shook her and beat her down, and another struck her to her knees. She struggled and writhed on the floor and at last she screamed hoarsely in labour.

Joe Saul rushed in. "Mordeen," he cried. He saw her twisting on the floor. He ran to her and gathered her against his breast. He raised his head and shouted: "Mr Victor! Mr Victor, hurry, goddam you! Victor, come help me!"

ACT THREE, SCENE II

THE CHILD

THE small square room was white, impersonal, undecorated, a cell, a little sterile box with a wide door on one side. And in its centre stood a high hospital bed and bedside table with a glass of water and a glass straw. And the room was muffled and silent, secret and cut off from every world.

Mordeen lay in the bed, her hair spread over the pillow, and a bundle, silent and covered, was beside her. Her face was masked with gauze and she lay very still, but her breathing was hoarse and her chest rose fiercely, struggling to bring a rush of pure air to her lungs. Then slowly her head turned from side to side and she muttered and moaned, fighting her way up from drugged unconsciousness.

The wide swing-door opened and he stood in the entrance. He wore cap and long white tunic. The face, except for the eyes, was covered with a surgical mask. He came softly round the bed and looked down at her under the soft night-light. And then he looked down at the muffled bundle that lay beside her. And his gloved hand gently pulled the covering aside.

"Mordeen," he said softly.

As though she heard him, she took a great gasp of air into her lungs and her head twisted from side to side. "Dead," she whispered. "Dead—the whole world—dead —Victor dead."

He said: "No, Mordeen, not dead—here and alive, always."

She threshed her head violently and she whimpered: "Friend Ed, I wanted—I wanted him to have his child. I wanted—but it's dead. Everything is dead."

Joe Saul said: "Listen to me, Mordeen. He is here—and resting. He's had great effort and now he's sleeping—a little wrinkled and very tired—and the soft hair——" He looked down. "And his mouth—the sweet mouth—like your mouth, Mordeen."

Her eyes snapped open and she struggled up. "Joe Saul, where are you? Joe Saul? Why did you go? Where did you go?"

He pressed her back against the pillow and took a cloth from the table and dried her wet forehead.

"I'm here, Mordeen. I didn't go away, or, if I did, I came back. I'm here."

And she muttered: "Who is dead? Is Joe Saul dead?"

"I'm here," he said. "I went away into an insanity, but now I'm back."

"Maybe he'll never know," she said secretly. "Maybe he'll never guess. Maybe Joe Saul will be content." Her chest contracted and she held her breath.

He wiped her forehead until her throat relaxed. "Rest," he said. "I do know and I know more. I know that what seemed the whole tight pattern is not important. Mordeen, I thought, I felt, I knew that my particular seed had importance over other seed. I thought that was what I had to give. It is not so. I know it now."

She said: "You are Joe Saul? Faceless—only a voice and a white facelessness."

"I thought my blood must survive—my line—but it's not so. My knowledge, yes—the long knowledge remembered, repeated, the pride, yes, the pride and warmth, Mordeen, warmth and companionship and love so that the loneliness we wear like icy clothes is not always there. These I can give."

"Where is your face?" she asked. "What's happened to your face, Joe Saul?"

"It's not important. Just a face. The eyes, the nose, the shape of chin—I thought they were worth preserving because they were mine. It is not so.

"It is the race, the species that must go staggering on.

154

Mordeen, our ugly little species, weak and ugly, torn with insanities, violent and quarrelsome, sensing evil—the only one that senses cleanness and is dirty, that knows about cruelty and is unbearably cruel."

She tried to sit up, tried to raise herself. "Joe Saul, the baby was born dead."

"The baby is alive," he said. "This is the only important thing. Be still, Mordeen. Lie quietly and rest. I've walked into some kind of hell and out. The spark continues—a new human—only being of its kind anywhere —that has struggled without strength when every force of tooth and claw, of storm and cold, of lightning and germ was against it—struggled and survived, survived even the self-murdering instinct."

"Where is he?" she asked.

"Look down. Here he lies sleeping, to teach me. Our dear race, born without courage but very brave, born with a flickering intelligence and yet with beauty in its hands. What animal has made beauty, created it, save only we? With all our horrors and our faults, somewhere in us there is a shining. That is the most important of all facts. *There is a shining.*"

Her eyes were clearing now and her brain climbed up out of the grey ether cloud. "You are Joe Saul," she said. "You are my husband—and you know?"

"I know," he said. "I had to walk into the black to know —to know that every man is father to all children and every child must have all men as father. This is not a little piece of private property, registered and fenced and separated. Mordeen! This is *the Child.*"

Mordeen said: "It is very dark. Turn up the light. Let me have light. I cannot see your face."

"Light," he said. "You want light? I will give you light." He tore the mask from his face, and his face was shining and his eyes were shining. "Mordeen," he said, "I love the child." His voice swelled and he spoke loudly. "Mordeen, I love our child." And he raised his head and cried in triumph, "Mordeen, *I love my son.*"

One of the greatest American writers
of this century, winner of the
1962 Nobel Prize for Literature

John Steinbeck

Uninhibited in his choice of material,
insatiably curious about the human race,
Steinbeck is also a natural story-teller.
The sinewy strength and realistic harshness
of his writing, lit by flashes of humour and
poetry, make unforgettable reading.

THE PEARL and BURNING BRIGHT 3/6
THE LOG FROM THE SEA OF CORTEZ 5/-
SWEET THURSDAY 3/6
THE WINTER OF OUR DISCONTENT 5/-
TRAVELS WITH CHARLEY 5/-
EAST OF EDEN 7/6

'That tremendous genius, John Steinbeck'
H. G. WELLS

'One of those novelists—they are growing fewer—who have never forgotten that the primary aim of the novel is to tell a story, to tell it interestingly and to tell it convincingly.'

NICHOLAS MONSARRAT

Castle Garac 3/6

A Literary Guild Choice, this is the first British edition.

'An exciting story in the tradition of Daphne du Maurier's *Rebecca*.'

Other books available in Pan:
SOMETHING TO HIDE 3/6
THE TIME BEFORE THIS 2/6
SMITH AND JONES 2/6
THE STORY OF ESTHER COSTELLO 3/6
A FAIR DAY'S WORK 3/6
THE SHIP THAT DIED OF SHAME 3/6
THE PILLOW FIGHT 5/-

ALEC WAUGH

THE MULE ON THE MINARET   7/6

Against a background of luxurious living in
Beirut's palaces, spartan living in Baghdad and
adventures in Cairo and Damascus, the author
draws from his own experience in British
Intelligence for this exciting novel.

'... bursting with colour and movement'
Evening News

'... adventure, sex, exotic setting — red-hot
readability'   *Books and Bookmen*

ISLAND IN THE SUN   7/6

A world bestseller, filmed by Twentieth
Century-Fox with a star-studded cast, a
tremendous story of intrigue, murder and
passion — on a sun-drenched tropical island.

'The story ... of love, lust, murder, political
intrigue and social eruption ... superbly
executed and always gripping ... the pace is
terrific'   *Evening News*

FUEL FOR THE FLAME   6/-

Passions flare in the conflicts between
people — dark-skinned and white — in this
powerful novel set on the imaginary island of
Karak in the South China Sea.

'Sophisticated and sensitive ... his book is a
marvellously good companion'   *Daily Mail*